About The Author

Steven J Yeo is a playwright and novelist based in Bristol, England. He has several plays, comedy farces, and pantomimes being licensed and performed all over the world.

His first series of novels is the *Keterlyn* series, which is horror based. The first of these published at the end of 2022, and further books in the series, are being released and reprinted in 2024.

Other books by Seven J Yeo

Keterlyn

Teaching Keterlyn

Queenie Escapes

Queenie in France

Queenie in England (2025)

Catch 212

Dad's Island

By

Steven J Yeo

Chapter One

"Get your feet off the table," came the roar through my office door. "And get back to work." It was Michael Hamilton the second. A young executive who has just taken over the role of C.E.O. from his much-loved and respected father. I ignored him, turned the page of my book, and continued reading.

"Did you hear what I said?" he screamed through the office door.

"Who didn't?" I remarked back, without taking my eyes from my book. He often made efforts to assert his dominance in the workplace, a challenge given his consistent errors and a novice's understanding of the job. But he seemed to have some notion that I needed 'executive guidance', as he called it. I hoped he would notice the time and just walk away.

The office layout fell short to avoid those brief confrontations with the boy wonder. The four 'workers' doors, as I like to refer to us, all faced the expansive office suite of our recently appointed C.E.O. Graciously leaving us workers sharing prison cell sized, six feet by ten feet, offices with our assistants.

"Well?" he continued.

Perhaps not. I gave him a hint.

"Michael, I am on my lunch break." I lifted my head from my book and looked at the clock on the wall opposite me. "I have forty-five minutes left, Michael."

He realised he was in the wrong and stammered, yet again.

"Well, well, get your feet off the table," he added.

"No," I replied and continued to read.

"Are, are, are, are you going to ignore a direct order from me?"

"Yes, I are. Now fuck off, Michael, and tell somebody who actually gives a shit."

He stormed off down the corridor. I had no idea about his destination in his embarrassed, stammering condition, since it was Saturday, and I was the sole foolish person who volunteered to fill in during holidays. Volunteered; I mean subjected to banal hints and observations all week until I said I'd cover another accountants means of escaping the humdrum existence of working here.

The new company policy stated that our assistants had to follow the same working hours as us. So poor Janie had to give up her Saturday off with her ageing father and new boyfriend, to assist me with work that I could quite easily have completed unaided. She'd be back from the Cornish pasty shop at any minute, and we'd eat lunch together.

I'm not saying she wasn't good at her job, on the contrary. Her fastidiousness in our tasks is a valuable trait for accountants. A few times, she has helped me avoid trouble with my final tallies. She was in her thirties, with dark hair and hazel eyes, and I thought she was very pretty, poetic, but I think I missed my chance of romance with her by being too shy at the start of our affiliation. She had finally met her dream man, and he was her constant topic of conversation, and I happily listened to her tales of her weekends with Morris, hoping to find cracks in their relationship to get a foot in.

I can't speak with any expertise about romance. I've never had a wife, kids, or even a steady girlfriend. Life slipped away. In my forties, my life experiences have been limited to what I've seen on TV or in movies. My mother died ten years ago, about a year after all the turmoil with my father and the divorce. When he left the military, she said he was impossible to live with. Our relationship is okay now, but Father and I rarely see each other.

Once my adopted brother found love in Italy, he left home immediately. They stayed together until his death around two years ago. We always kept in touch and spent Christmas together most years.

I sensed Janie was close; the air filled with the smell of the pasties. We always left the office door open for air circulation. Our masters, the Hamiltons, never justified the expense of air conditioning or heating systems in the winter months. So, we left the front door open for air con in summer, and huddled around expensive Calor gas heaters when required, in the winter. Thankfully, the Hamiltons were not as bad as Ebeneezer Scrooge, although I paid for my gas bottle refills.

Janie entered, carrying one bag from the Cornish pasty shop and one from Gregg's. She bought us a cake as well.

She closed the office door, placed the two bags on her desk, sitting opposite mine and below the clock, then returned to the door to hang up her coat. I closed my book and slid it into my desk drawer.

We have a wall of windows facing the lord and masters' office windows, but I carefully positioned all the filing cabinets against them so at least I only had to look at the boss when he walked past our window or stuck his head in when the door was open.

"I smelled them a mile off." I said to her.

"Sorry it took so long. I had to queue at both shops today. Saturday shoppers I s'pect."

She walked back to her desk, sat on her chair, and fetched a paper bag from inside the carrier and passed it to me.

"We've got pudding too, if you eat all your dinner," she said with a smile, sitting at her desk. She tried to mother me a bit in the office, and I was happy to let her take care of me as much as she liked.

With our desks opposite each other, we both faced a different wall, but it allowed us to scoot our office chairs to each other to pass across paperwork or ask specific questions pertaining to work, or to share food.

We both loved the pasties from the Cornish pasty shop. We felt rewarded when working overtime on a Saturday. They improved our mood to come in on our day off.

With pasties devoured, I poured the coffee while she tore bags to give us both a kind of serving plate for our cherry topped iced buns.

"These are not good for my diet," she stated as she placed one bun on my desk.

"You don't need to diet Janie," I told her. "If that boyfriend of yours keeps telling you that you're fat, he has shit in his eyes and you need to get shot of him."

"But he is right. I have put on loads of weight since we met," she said.

"That is what normal couples call contentment. Lots of new couples gain a few pounds. Don't believe him, it's just one of those things."

It seems like Janie's boyfriend is turning into a narcissist. I noticed her stories with her girlfriends were becoming less frequent, spending more time with him instead. I was worried.

Her dress sense had also changed over those last couple of months. Previously, she dressed provocatively and attracted attention. However, lately she dressed more conservatively, like her mother would. I wonder if it's related to her new boyfriend. It wasn't cold enough to hide so much. I promised myself to keep an eye on things.

As the 'dick' strictly prohibits drinks, we adopted a certain way of drinking coffee in our office. A false filing cabinet with a drop front served as a tray. Inside, we hid the coffee maker, condiments, and mugs from prying eyes. We scooted our chairs to the window filing cabinets and drank with our backs to the window. Our presence was invisible to our 'master' unless he opened the door and entered. By then, we stowed our cups and concealed everything in the filing cabinet. It sounds pathetic, but it was the path of least resistance. Until I found a job where Janie could work alongside me, we had to endure it.

The next hour dragged until the office front door slammed, and I heard voices in the hallway. I peered over the top of one filing cabinet, and I saw it was that new client of Michaels'. A right dodgy looking character if you asked me. Every time, he appeared with a pair of minders or bodyguards, all clad in expensive suits. I certainly had seen his face before, but I couldn't put my finger on where. Anyway, he looked familiar to me. I had doubts about whether the profit would be greater than the cost when his only son and heir tried to prove to his father that he can attract new business to the company. But that was up to him; I stayed the hell out of it. I was certain that Old man Hamilton wouldn't have associated with him.

Janie spoke, and I shushed her on her first syllable.

"Shh. Stay down! Don't let them know we are here." I whispered to her. "That's his new client again, the one who looks like a mafia boss."

We heard the discussion getting heated, and the voices became more audible.

"I told you that these investments will take time. You'll have to be patient." Michael appeared to be asserting his dominance with his tone. I had doubts about whether this client was the best choice.

"The only thing you had to do was clean the money, not re-invest again. Deposit it into the company accounts and repay me. I'm giving you a five percent cut for essentially not doing anything," said his client.

"Marco, my father would become suspicious if all I did was pay money into our accounts and withdrawal it. I told you that at the beginning," stated Michael.

One large bodyguard glanced around. I had to duck before he noticed me. I ushered Janie to the end of the filing cabinets towards her desk.

"Let's get out of sight," I whispered, as I eased her into position behind the side of the filing cabinet.

"My coat, they will see my coat, and the bags," she whispered back.

I crouched down below the top of the cabinets and moved to the door. I reached up and grabbed her coat and returned to her, sweeping the carrier bags from the table as I passed.

"Are you alone today?" Marco asked.

"Of course I am," Michael replied.

That is the first righteous thing he had ever done. I peered over the cabinet in the corner and saw Marco take out a gun from his suit jacket. I ducked down again and looked at Janie.

"Stay down, he has a gun," I whispered, terrified to her.

Janie panicked, and I held her in my arms to calm her down a bit.

"It's ok. If we keep quiet and out of sight, we'll be fine," I assured her.

She calmed a little, and I peered out again.

"Transfer the balance of my account to this account number and do it now so I can check it's done," Marco demanded.

"But it has been invested elsewhere. I told you that," Michael pleaded.

"Then you are no good to me," Marco stated.

The gun firing in the office startled us. A chair and desk made noise while something heavy fell, scattering paperwork, before silence ensued.

We crouched behind the filing cabinet, hiding and trying to appear as small as possible. I held Janie in my arms so that we both occupied the same space available. She was shaking and had tears running down her face.

"Shh!" I pleaded with her.

She fought back against her sobs. She buried her face in my chest, trying hard not to make any sound.

"Check that he's alone," Marco commanded of the two men. Then I heard someone searching through filing cabinets, opening and closing drawer after drawer, with the occasional rustling of paperwork as each one got searched.

I stopped breathing when our office door opened. I think Janie did the same. I dared not look. I held onto Janie tight, as she buried her face into my chest. The door closed. Was he in the room moving towards us, or had he superficially looked and closed the empty office door behind him? I couldn't tell and continued to hold my breath. A few seconds passed and felt like an eternity. I let my breath go and quietly held another.

"There's no one here, boss." Came a gruff voice.

"Ok, let's get out of here. I have all the information I need," said Marco.

Michaels' office door closed, followed by footsteps, then the slamming of the front door. Janie and I maintained our position a little longer, waiting to hear if anyone stayed behind. After a brief silence, I released Janie.

"Are you alright?" I asked.

"I'm fine, but did he shoot Michael?"

I looked over the filing cabinets to Michael's room but saw nothing.

"You stay here. I'll look."

"Be careful," she added.

Slowly, I crept to the door and opened it quietly. I peered around the doorway and the hallway seemed clear. I stepped over to Michaels' office, and through the window, on the floor amongst some paperwork, with a bloody hole in the centre of his forehead sprawled Michael. I realized he was dead. I rushed to the front door and locked it so that no one entered. When I drew level with Michael's office door, Janie stepped out of our office.

"No, don't come out. I don't want you to see him."

"Is he…" she paused. "Is he dead?"

"Yes, he is."

It was at that point that I felt sorry for him. Yes, he was a dick, and pissed with his newfound power, but he didn't deserve this. Well, maybe he did. His involvement with Marco was a mistake from the beginning, but his death was undeserved.

"We need to call the police," I told Janie.

"But won't those men find out we hid here all the time?" she asked.

"That's in the movies Janie. In real life, it doesn't happen that way."

At least I hoped not. They say some movies are based on actual events, although they may be exaggerated and changed a little with its telling.

"There's no choice. It wouldn't take long for the police to find out that we were here all along. I will tell them that only I witnessed Marco shooting Michael," I told her.

"But I didn't see him shoot," she said.

"Then you have nothing to worry about."

"But I saw him in his office, and I heard the gunshot," she added. "I am as much in this as you are."

"I'll try to keep you out of it as much as I can, OK?" I tried to reassure her. "Now you make us a nice coffee and I'll call the police.

"Coffee! Who can think of coffee at a time like this?"

"Ok then. Go away, so you don't have to look at him in his condition while I call the police."

"His condition! He's dead. Someone shot him. It's not curable like the flu or measles."

She was getting herself worked up, understandably.

"Please make some coffee. It will help to calm you down a bit. Trust me. I need to call the police. Let's be a little respectful towards him. He did not deserve to die, did he?" I said.

She took a deep breath and a big sniff.

"You're right, call them."

She entered our office, and I heard her banging the filing cabinets and mugs. I retrieved my phone from my pocket. My God! What if one of us had had a text message or a call while they looked for us? We didn't think about our phones. I guess we were just lucky, if we can call witnessing a pointless murder as actually being lucky. Luck did not favour poor Michael. I really felt sorry for him and sorrier for his father for when he finds out about his only son and heir murdered for being business naïve and just trying to impress his father.

I looked at my phone screen. For a moment, I couldn't remember the number I needed to call. Maybe the event also shocked me. I was so busy trying to look after Janie I didn't give any thought to me being in a state of shock. Less shocked than Janie granted but shocked none the less. The moment soon passed, and I dialled 999.

Once the emergency operator heard the words gun and shot, everything seemed to happen quickly. Five or six police officers arrived within the first five minutes, with the armed response team about ten minutes after that. I'm not sure if the armed police came from a lot farther away, or if they were in no hurry, as the armed criminals had already fled the scene.

The police ushered Janie and me into different offices to give our statements of what had happened. Detective Inspector Moffatt questioned me. He was in his late fifties and dressed in a suit but looked unkempt with his unbrushed shoulder-length blonde hair. His suit looked as if he had slept in it overnight, although that should not show his detecting capabilities. Maybe it should. Time will tell in that instance; he could be another Columbo. He was an ex-family man, as he called himself. His ex-wife took everything from him in the brutal divorce proceedings. His collectable MGB GT in metallic red, his most prized possession, and of course all the savings, the house, and the kids. She must have poisoned the kids against him, as they never wanted to spend any time with him. Not that he ever had much time to give them, but when he did, they were always busy with their friends, or his ex-wife made sure they were too busy visiting her family.

His second in command was Detective Sergeant Wilkinson, who was in his thirties and a lot more aggressive than his mentor. He had something to prove. He knew that the D.I. retired soon in three or four years, and if he kept his nose clean and worked hard, he could be next in line for the position.

He talked to Janie, and I heard her getting more and more distraught as the conversation continued. I wanted to reassure her everything was alright, but I heard the detective getting louder questioning her, and I tried to hear both conversations. My God! Do these morons actually think *we* shot Michael?

"Inspector, by the sound of your sergeant next door, you think we did it and that we have hid the gun or something. Are you that stupid?" I asked him with my *'I'm better than you'* attitude.

"Currently, sir, we hold no opinions. We are just gathering information, that's all," he replied.

"Well, I suggest you tell that to the twat next door, before you have to arrest me for assaulting a police officer, when I smack him one. She was absolutely terrified when it happened, and he isn't helping at all," I told him.

The inspector looked sheepish. He knew I was right. His sergeant was going at her heavy-handed. He poked his head into the hallway and raised his voice.

"Sergeant, bring the witness in here, please. We'll question them together."

A few seconds later, a distraught Janie rushed into my arms full of tears.

"He was trying to get me to confess," she blubbered.

The inspector looked and scowled at his subordinate. I held Janie tight as she openly cried into my chest.

"I guess we're done here, inspector," I said.

"We're nowhere near done yet. Not until I say we're done the inspector asserted.

"No, we're done. If you need to speak to either of us, from now on, it will be with a solicitor," I said.

"Then I will have no other choice than to arrest you both under suspicion of murder."

"Careful inspector. A knee jerk reaction like that will cost you your job. I promise you it will. Your crime scenes investigators have swabbed us for gunpowder residue, which will come back clear. I am sure you have already found some C.C.T.V. footage of the three killers leaving the office and shopping centre dressed exactly as we described. So no, we will be on our way now. You have our addresses and contact details and if you ask us nicely, we may even come down to the station with our solicitors to continue this at a later date, when it is convenient for us, of course."

I didn't know I had that in me. Well played. I was trying hard not to smile at my masterful achievement. I led Janie to the door.

"My coat," she whispered.

I let her go at the door and went to the end filing cabinet where we hid from Marco and his boys. The sergeant blocked my path and refused to budge.

"Move!" I demanded, and he stepped to the side. I gathered Janie's coat and moved back to her. I put the coat around her shoulders and put my arm around her; she was still crying. What an ordeal it has been for her; well, for both of us, really.

Stepping out of the office, we encountered reporters near the yellow police tape. I, for one, wanted no more questions today, and I knew Janie was in no shape to answer them.

"Are you the deceased's wife or girlfriend?" One insensitive asshole yelled across to us. Janie dug in deeper to my chest, trying not to look at them. I just looked in amazement at them. How could they be so insensitive? There were also members of the public gathered with their phones in the air, recording everything. My God, what has this world come to? I suppose we will be on YouTube and I.T.V. west country news later. It may even make the B.B.C.

A thought quickly crossed my mind. Until now, Marco thought there were no witnesses. If I don't say something, he will assume we were. I stopped dead in my tracks at the edge of the curb and a taxi pulled up. I opened the door for Janie to get in and turned to the reporters.

"All I will say is, that we discovered a colleague's body. It's been very upsetting. Please respect our need for privacy. Thank you."

As I climbed into the taxi, I heard the voices shouting out to get more information from me.

"Who is the deceased?"

"Was he murdered?"

I ignored them and closed the car door.

"I'll take you home first Janie."

The taxi driver pulled away. "Where to?" he asked.

"Begbroke road, Frenchay, please," I said.

"I don't want to be by myself," Janie blurted.

"Ok, then let's go to mine after you grab some clothes and toothbrush or whatever, for your stay. I have a spare room you can use."

"Thank you Bruce. For everything," she whispered, so that the driver didn't hear.

"No worries. We both deserve a strong drink after this."

It took about six minutes to pull up outside Janie's house.

"That'll be nine quid forty please?" the driver asked.

I leant forward to pay him and I noticed that Janie's front door was open.

"I don't want to alarm you, but do you usually leave your front door open?"

"No, why?" She leant across me. Suddenly, she panicked again. "Oh no. Have they found us already?"

From being relaxed, she was immediately thrust back into her previous emotional state.

"Quick drive, move away. Just go!" I said, prodding the driver's back.

He sped away, and I looked behind us for any signs of Marco and his boys following us.

"Shit! Shit, shit, shit," I cussed.

"What are we going to do?" Janie asked.

"Let's not go to my place, just in case," I said. "I know! Drive, take us to the Rankin hotel in Bath, please. I have plenty of cash."

"No worries. I can see your lady is distressed. Relax, I can't see anyone following us," he said in his foreign accent.

It did relax, well, me anyway. Janie kept looking out the back window with tears in her eyes.

"Hey, you said the Rankin hotel. You have the same name. Anything I should know?" Janie asked, a little surprised.

"It's my brother's place. Well, adopted brother. He's dead now, but his wife Costanza keeps it running in his memory. I pay for a suite there to help maintain the place. Right now, I can't think of any other place to go," I said. "It was called the Rankin long before they bought it. They never had to change the name. So, I doubt anyone will know about it," I added.

A half hour later we pulled into the carpark of the Rankin. Janie experienced a significant decrease in restlessness. Less shocked and less stressed.

"No one followed us, pal," the driver said.

"Thank you. What do I owe you?" I asked.

"It's just over thirty pounds but call it thirty dead," he replied.

"We'll call it forty if you can promise not to tell anyone where we are. Not even your control."

"Sure, thing pal."

I pulled out my wallet from my suit jacket and gave him two twenty-pound notes.

"Can I have a receipt, please?" I ask.

Janie tutted.

"Yes, forget the receipt, old habits. Come on, let's get you that drink I promised you."

I grabbed one of his cards from the pocket in the back. You never know, we may need him again. Janie and I exited the cab.

The Rankin Hotel was a huge Bath stone-built house that got converted many years ago into the hotel that it is today. It had its own grounds with a carpark that could accommodate about six or seven cars at capacity. It looked like the hotel side of the street was where all the larger houses were. Some of them had been converted into B&Bs and hotels. The opposite side of the road appeared to have smaller studios, flats, and private residences, all made of the same Bath stone. It was certainly the more affordable side. The driver pulled away and drove out of the carpark.

"Give me your phone."

She passed it to me, and I removed the battery and the sim card and destroyed them as best I could. I also did the same with mine.

"We don't want them tracking us," I added, passing back her useless phone.

We crossed the gravelled carpark to the front of the hotel and climbed the steps to the open front doors and entered; we saw the reception desk. Costanza stood there, behind the old desk, with her head buried in paperwork. She was a lot older than my brother Grahame was. She was originally from Italy and was a beautiful soul. I fully understood why he loved her so much. Her white hair in a big bun made her look more like a granny than a hotel owner. She also had the most fascinating green eyes. When I saw them, I couldn't help but gaze at them repeatedly. She saw me and was about to give her *'how may I help you'* speech, but immediately reacted to my presence with a big, beautiful smile.

"Brucey. Brucey, Brucey," she said, all the way from the back of the reception desk, with her arms held open. She gave me the warmest, friendliest hug I had had in quite a while. Maybe since we last met.

"Hello Costanza. How are things?" I asked.

"Good, all is good. And you look wonderful, and you have finally got a real-life girlfriend. Welcome, welcome," she said, giving Janie a hug.

"Costanza, this is Janie, my assistant at work. Janie this is Costanza, my brother's widow. She gives the best hugs in the world."

Janie smiled and reciprocated, a little embarrassed.

"You stay for dinner?" Costanza asked.

"We'll stay for a few days, if that's okay?" I stated.

"You have a dirty weekend, yes?" Costanza added.

"God, no Costanza. Please prepare both rooms in my suite. Or two single rooms if it is not available, please," I said with a smile.

Janie bowed her head with embarrassment.

"I thought it was too good to be true. No woman is ever good enough for our Brucey," Costanza pointed out. "I need nieces and nephews. When will I finally have bambinos to spoil?" she asked, touching both of my cheeks.

"One day Costanza, one day," I told her.

"First hell would have frozen over, I think," Costanza added soulfully. "Franco, Franco," she called out.

A small wiry man in his sixties promptly appeared.

"My Brucey and his ragazza will stay in suite numero uno," she instructed. "Get it ready and go fetch their luggage from the car."

"We have no luggage, Costanza, just us," I added.

"Oh, I see," she said.

"I'll explain later."

"I will have little Margarite make up both beds for you. "Come, enjoy food and drinks while we prepare everything," said Costanza, guiding us to the dining and bar area.

"Thank you, Costanza," said Janie, gaining a little more confidence.

"Anything for my Brucey and his ragazza," said Costanza, leading the way.

"What is ragazza?" Janie asked me quietly, so Costanza didn't hear.

"I'm not sure. When we're settled, I'll google it."

Chapter Two

Settle, we did. The risotto proved to be the best I have ever tasted. Even Janie, who said she was not that keen on it before she ate, devoured her plate full. Washed down with a copious amount of wine; I had stuffed myself to the brim. The same sensation I used to have as a kid when my mother had cooked one of her famous roast dinners with meat and five veg.

Janie had yawned halfway through dinner. She needed to retire for the night. So, I made our excuses and led her upstairs to my suite. I showed her to the twin bedroom, and I had my usual double bedroom. I had scrounged a couple of new toothbrushes and toothpaste from Costanza, which she sold to all the guests who had forgotten the basics, and she even lent Janie a nightdress. It looked old-fashioned, but it seemed better than nothing. We said goodnight and went to our separate rooms.

I must have led there for an hour, contemplating the day's events. Yet, one unanswered question remained in my head. How did Marco and his mob find out about us so fast? He probably knew before we reached Janie's, a journey that lasted only six minutes. Her open front door might not have been for that reason, but it was too coincidental to ignore.

The floor creaked, and I heard a rustling beside my bed. It startled me and I sat up to see what it was. There stood Janie in her old lady nightdress, looking puzzled.

"Oh, you scared me," I said to her. "What's the matter? You look worried?"

"Sorry, I didn't mean to scare you, but may I ask you something?"

"Sure," I moved across under the blankets so she could sit on it. Instead, she climbed in next to me and leaned against the headboard the same as me. I got a little flustered as I sleep naked, and there was nothing to hide my modesty as she climbed inside the covers. She didn't seem phased at all.

"How did they learn about us and how did they find out so quickly?" she asked.

I smiled.

"First, we don't actually, a hundred percent, know it was them at your house. But I'm sure it was. I don't believe in coincidences. And, yes, how did they react so quick? I'm lying here trying to answer that myself."

"Do you think one of the police told them?"

"A bent copper? That wouldn't surprise me. That is the only explanation I can come up with, too."

I turned to face her and tucked the sheets into me to hide my nudity.

"I mean, they left and presumably went home or back to their headquarters or whatever baddies do, right? It took us at least five minutes to get settled and another six or seven for the police to arrive. So even if they only got ten minutes away; if they had to turn around and head to yours, that only leaves a few minutes either way. So, they had to have been told by someone," I said.

"I agree. Nothing else fits the timeline." She paused and turned to face me more and posed herself, unnaturally. "So, what are we going to do?"

"We must inform the police about the danger of going back home. But if we do, are we telling the mole?"

"It could be the inspector," she interjected.

"Exactly! And does that mean we have to go into hiding?"

"How long will that be?" she asked.

"Until they catch them and send them to prison."

"But that might take years," she said, creasing her forehead.

We sat, exchanging worried glances, for a few minutes. I saw her eyes welling up with tears. I didn't want her to cry again.

"First things first. We are safe tonight," I said. "No one, except the taxi driver, knows we are here. So, let's get a good night's sleep and we'll decide what to do in the morning."

I looked at her, expecting her to climb out of my bed, but she never moved.

"Can I stay here tonight? I'm still a little scared, to be honest."

Now I wished Costanza had given me some old pyjamas.

"Alright," I said. "Night, night."

I turned away from her and led down, trying to allow the sheets to fall in-between us. She did the same, and I thought that I may sleep tonight when she suddenly sat up. I rolled onto my back.

"What's the matter?" I asked, expecting her to say that she had realised something that I hadn't.

"This nightdress smells of mothballs," she said, pulling the front to her nose.

It caused me to chuckle, and I rolled back onto my side. The bed jostled and bounced a little.

"That's better," she said. "Aw, but now I'm cold."

The next thing I knew, was her soft hands gently embrace me and her naked body pressed against mine. It felt wonderful to me.

"Is that better?" I asked.

There was a brief pause.

"No, turn over. I want to see your smile. I know you are smiling."

She was right, of course I was smiling. All my Christmases had come early. I had been eagerly anticipating and dreaming of this moment for months. I turned over to look at her, and her smile was intoxicating. She touched my face and was about to kiss me.

"What about Morris?" I asked her, still smiling.

"He didn't save my life today. You did. You deserve me. He doesn't," she stated.

"Can't argue with that logic," I said, and our lips met.

The warm softness of her body invigorated my tired and stressed body as my hands moved over her. The more I touched her, the more she moaned with delight. With each new part of her skin that I touched, she shivered. The more she shivered, the more my stiffness awakened me. She started pulling me to mount her. I climbed between her legs, and they opened to accommodate me. I resisted the urge to rush. I wanted nothing more at that precise moment than to penetrate her. I sensed she wanted the same.

Instead, I kissed her and allowed my kisses to move across her breasts and down her body, until they found the moistness and centre of her pleasure. I darted my tongue in and out of her and relished the sticky creases and folds of her skin. She allowed me to investigate her for a few minutes longer, before her breathing became faster and sharper. She gently pulled on my ears to bring my head back into view. I continued to kiss all the way up her soft body until once again our lips met and our tongues danced with each other.

She wanted me to enter her, and again I resisted. It's been years since I experienced love like this. I refused to rush. If I surrendered, it would have been over in a few quick strokes.

She forcibly turned me onto my back, and I knew she was going to do the work herself. I closed my eyes and prepared to be mounted. Suddenly, her mouth and her tongue started licking and caressing me. Drinking the stickiness and trying to suck more out of me. I wanted to explode, and nothing was going to stop me. I had no control over anything. I made so much noise I thought Costanza would hear us downstairs.

Amongst my outbursts, a little disappointed moan came from Janie. I promptly moved her away and positioned myself on top while still firm enough. The movement of our bodies together increased my rigidness to full capacity again, and I helped her reach the same point I had reached a few moments before. The sound of her moaning and the jerking of her body was beautiful. She jerked again and again, as I moved slower inside of her. She wrapped her legs around my waist, and we soon shared one huge, uncontrollable, orgasmic moment together, for what felt like an eternity. Then slowly we jerked less and moved less until she untied her legs from me, and I rolled off her. We were both panting and breathing heavily.

I had wanted that moment for months. Ever since, she joined as my assistant. I daydreamed about her in the office and had visually undressed her frequently. I was a shy gentleman, particularly with the opposite sex. But nothing measured up to the real thing. All the stress from the day's events disappeared, leaving me happy and fulfilled. I hoped she felt the same way, too.

We slept peacefully, clutching each other until morning noises from the hotel check-outs disturbed me. I had slept through the night for the first time in quite a while. Janie was still asleep when I woke. She was resting on my chest with her arm around me. I glanced at her, gently brushing her hair aside to see her sleeping face. In that moment, she was beautiful, and I was the luckiest man alive. She stirred and her eyes looked up at me and that infectious smile crept across her lips.

"Morning," she smiled.

"Morning. You better today?"

"Oh, yes, much better," she said, stretching her arms and arching her back, removing any remnants of sleep from her body.

"I need a shower, I said and stood in all my nakedness, moving towards the bathroom. She caught hold of my arm.

"You need someone to wash your back?" she asked with that same smile on her face.

"Um, yes, but I think it is impractical here. It's a tiny shower cubicle. I'll put it on my list for renovations. Wasn't important until now."

With a disappointed expression, she released my arm.

"Oh, ok," she said, enjoying another stretch on the big empty double bed.

I stepped into the small shower cubicle and closed the glass door. It was tiny; hardly enough room to swing a cat, as my mother would have said. At least the water was hot and invigorating. I could hear Janie saying something from the other room.

"What?" I called out.

She stepped into the doorway of the bathroom.

"I said, what time is breakfast? My God, you weren't joking about the telephone booth shower," and laughed.

"Yes, I said it was tiny. Costanza will do us something whatever time we want it. The kitchen here is open all day for guests."

She pointed towards the toilet. "May I?" she asked.

"Sure."

I couldn't believe she was going to use the toilet in front of me. Even if we were married, that is still something I couldn't have done. I was wrong. She closed the toilet lid and sat on it, crossing her legs. The shower cubicle was now within her reach, and she started drawing a smiley face on the steamy glass.

"Any thoughts on what we're gonna do?" she asked.

I lathered myself with the body wash Costanza gave me, but in that tiny shower cubicle, the water was washing the suds from me as fast as I could rub it on. It didn't help me with Janie sat there naked with her pert little breasts on show. It was all I could do to stop myself from showing my sexual interest in her peaking again. I turned away from her and continued to lather myself.

"We have to inform the police. At least then our houses can be made secure by them. And I think we should only talk to the inspector; he is most likely to be straight."

"How can you say that?" she asked.

"Simple. He looked as if he slept in that suit of his. His shoes were badly scuffed, and he had no flashy watch or anything. It is unlikely that he gets extra money from other sources."

"Ok. So, what? We call him, or turn up at the station?"

"I think it best we call him. As that way, no one will get a chance at us on the way there or on the way back."

"Ok. If you're sure, then that's what we will do," she added.

"I'm not sure. But the police have got to be more used to this stuff than we are. Perhaps they will place us in protective custody. Or put a guard on us for protection. I don't know, I'm winging it."

"As long as we're together." She paused. "We are together now, aren't we?"

"In this murder stuff, yes. But if you want to be together, together, then you'll have to get rid of Morris," I stated, turning to look her in the eyes.

As I saw her, the smiley face she had drawn on the glass cubicle was correctly positioned to replace her face. It must have looked the same from her viewpoint, and we both smiled at it.

"As long as you are not just using me," she added.

"Using you?" I turned the shower off. "You came on to me last night, remember?"

"I know, but you have been so fucking slow. I've been there for months, but even when I faked having a boyfriend, you took no action."

I stepped from the shower and on to the thick fluffy mat. I took the towel from the rail beside her and dried myself.

"I am slow and shy, I know. Always have been. But when I was ready to make a move, your boyfriend appeared, and I just assumed I had missed my chance. Wait a minute, you said faked?"

She paused and stood. There was only a towel between us.

"I was trying to make you jealous so you would become interested," she said, wrapping her arms around my waist.

"So, you lied to me."

"I bent the truth a little."

She raised her hand and made a small gap between her thumb and forefinger to show how little it was and smiled. How could anybody not fall into that infectious smile of hers? I kissed her, and she returned the gesture.

"Am I forgiven?" she asked, removing the towel from me and dropping it to the floor. Now, there was nothing between us.

"No! I mean, yes, I forgive you. But no, not that now. We must get some breakfast and sort things out with the inspector."

I kissed her again.

"Go get ready and I'll reach out to the inspector to get things started. I'm gonna call him from the payphone across the street, just in case."

"Ok. Don't be long. I'll miss you while you're gone," she said.

I picked up the towel from the floor and laid it out flat.

"There's another towel on the rail. You can use this one to stand on if you like. Just leave them on the floor when you've finished and Margarite will replace them during the day, when she cleans the room."

"Thank you," she said and prepared for her shower.

I dressed fairly quickly but did struggle with my shirt, as I had forgotten to dry my back properly. My feet too. I had to borrow a phone card from Costanza to use the payphone. It took me three attempts to contact Inspector Moffatt. I didn't want to talk on the phone while he was in the station and asked for his mobile number to call him back later. Plus, I wanted to keep things short in case anyone was tracking his calls. With that done, I headed back to the hotel and Janie.

Chapter Three

Janie was dressed and waiting in the hotel reception area when I returned. She and Constanza smiled and greeted me with the air of a conspiracy happening. It felt a little unsettling.

"Welcome back. Costa is about to serve us some breakfast," said Janie.

"Costa? Since when did you two become close enough to use nicknames?" I replied with a smile. "And I have only been gone twenty minutes."

"Your ragazza is a wonderful lady, Brucey. You are lucky to have each other. My Michael would have loved her too," Costanza said.

I held her arm and looked at Janie. I led Costanza into the dining area, closely followed by a smiling Janie. "I miss him too Costa," I said and received a clip around the back of my head from Costanza.

"You call me Costanza," she said.

"But... but..." I yammered.

"Not as cute when you say it," said Costanza, to the amusement of Janie.

It was great they got on. Nice to have some joviality with us all. Her long-time husband Michael's death posed a significant challenge for her. He did everything for her and the hotel. Michael loved to be of service, always handled everything effortlessly, both in business and in social life. Going above and beyond for any of his customers. Even getting a foreign newspaper for them with some prior notice. If they asked for locations to the best restaurants and cafes, he would direct them or call them a taxi and instruct the driver himself of the destination. He also frequently took Costanza back home to Naples to see her family and especially her little sister, allowing her to stay for long periods and manage the hotel on his own. Michael gave it everything he had to run a tight ship, including all the maintenance work, running the bar, and outsourcing the accounts and advertising, allowing Costanza to run the kitchen; what she did best. So, when he died, she had no idea how to run the hotel. Since all of their money had been invested in the hotel, which also served as their residence, she needed to ensure its success. It had to be a success. I took charge of the finances for her, and we fought for a year to make it profitable. The hotel's careful investments have ensured a worry-free future with a steady income.

The continental breakfast was fantastic, as always. She served the coffee in traditional Italian demitasse cups. Tiny little expresso coffee cups. It's the little touches that keep visitors coming back.

Time was running out for our meeting with the inspector at the Royal Baths. I selected a public area for ample witnesses in case of any incident. We thanked Costanza for her splendid hospitality, and I told her we may be back to stay another night, or we may not depending on what happens with the inspector. She actually looked sad for us to go, and I was sure a tear appeared in her eye as we climbed into the taxi.

I told the driver quietly where we needed to go, to hide the destination from Costanza and thought it would be better if she was less involved.

I had forgotten how close the Rankin was to the Royal Baths; we should have walked. But I suppose arriving by car did mean no one had a chance to spot us on route if they had found out about our meeting today. The inspector was already there at the bottom of the steps, and Sergeant Wilkinson waited at the entrance to the visitor area at the top of the steps. I got the driver to drive onto Stall street just past where the Royal Baths were, and we got out. I had a good look around before moving towards the waiting police.

The inspector wore the same clothes as yesterday, as if he had slept in them. He greeted us with a limp handshake and ushered us up the steps towards his sergeant.

"You keep an eye outside for me please," the inspector instructed.

The sergeant reluctantly obeyed the orders. Janie and I followed the inspector onto the terrace which overlooked the historic Roman Baths. The three of us halted, peering over the balcony to the water beneath.

"The only answer I have is that they found out. I'm not sure how. If we have a mole, then I'm not sure who it is yet," the inspector quietly said to me.

I turned the inspector to face me. "Is it you?" I asked him, looking deep into his eyes. I could always tell if someone was lying to me by the look in their eyes. Well, mostly. It is not something I got much practice with, but on the whole I like to pride myself on the assumption that I could tell.

"No, and it won't ever be." he pulled out an envelope from his pocket and handed it to me.

"Here are some photos of Marcos' gang. Let me know who fired the shot and who was present, and I'll take care of the rest."

I showed Janie the envelope, unsure of what she had seen. I shuffled through the images and found the two guards, but not the killer.

"These two were there, but I don't see the one with the gun." I passed the photos across to him.

"Okay. One more," he said, retrieving another envelope from his other inside jacket pocket. He handed it to me.

There was only one picture inside. I took out the photo and there he was. The man with the gun, the one who killed Michael.

"Yes, that's him. He shot Michael."

"Are you sure?"

"Of course, I am sure. It scared us to death."

"My God. We better get you into protective custody. That is the big man himself. Marco Dellucci, third generation mobster. Finally, we can put him away," the inspector said delightedly.

"How bad is he?" Janie asked.

"He runs all the drugs, prostitution, and gambling for the whole of Bristol and surrounding areas, including here in Bath, and who knows where else? We need to get you somewhere safe. If someone can I.D. him, he'll stop at nothing to see them dead," the inspector instructed.

"Oh, that's just perfect," I said.

"Come on, let's get you somewhere safe," the inspector said.

We descended the steps onto Stall street, and I could see that his sergeant was on his mobile phone talking to someone. I reached out and grabbed the inspector's shoulder to stop him.

"Who is he talking to?" and pointed to his second in command.

"Let's find out."

He grabbed the phone from Sergeant Wilkinson and looked at it. He then spoke.

"Hi Sally, Tom Moffatt, just wanted to say hi. We see little of you these days," he said and waited with his ear to the phone. He smiled. "That would be nice, thank you. See you soon. I'll pass you back to Mike. Bye love, bye."

He passed the phone back to an indignant sergeant, who continued his conversation. "Let me call you back later, honey," he said, then put the phone into his pocket. "What was that about?" he asked the inspector.

"Moles and vermin Wilko, moles and vermin," the inspector said, increasing his pace.

"You thought I was the mole?" Wilkinson stated.

"Someone is. Don't let it get to you," the inspector instructed.

We walked briefly up Stall street to the inspectors' car, illegally parked on some zig-zag lines. A traffic warden was writing a ticket. The inspector removed his badge and showed the warden. The warden also removed a badge from his own pocket and showed the inspector, then ripped the ticket from his pad and pushed the ticket to the inspector's chest. The inspector held the ticket against his chest, then rolled it into a ball and threw it at the traffic warden.

"Fucking meter maids, pissed with power. I'll see you back at the station two, seven, three." The number on his shoulder epaulette.

"Bite me," came the swift reply.

"Does he know who you are?" I asked the inspector.

"He's my nephew, actually. He's pissed off he didn't get into the police force. I was the one who black balled him."

"Why did you black ball him?" asked a surprised Janie.

"'cus he's a useless druggie, and has no right being in any position of authority, as you're asking," the inspector scoffed and opened the rear car door for Janie and me to enter. His sergeant climbed into the front driver's seat with the inspector in the passenger seat. Then we sped off across the centre of Bath and it's ridiculous one-way system and onto the A36 towards Bristol. I saw where we were going and didn't like it.

"If you are heading to Bristol to protect us, you can forget it. It only took them six minutes to find us last time," I stated.

"We are not," the inspector said.

"We're not?" questioned Wilkinson.

"No, we're not. Actually, this will do. Pull over here to the garage," the inspector instructed.

Wilkinson steered the car into the garage and stopped at one of the pumps.

"Fill us up please, full tank," the inspector asked.

The sergeant complied with the request. Upon entering the shop to pay for the fuel, the inspector switched seats in the front. When the sergeant came back, the inspector wound down the driver's window to greet his return.

"You get a taxi back to the station from here. I'll drop these two off safe and meet you back there in about an hour," The inspector instructed and started the engine.

"But sir..?"

"Thank you sergeant."

We drove away from the garage in the opposite direction, back towards Kelston and Bath.

"So where are we going, inspector?" Janie asked.

"Oh, please, can you both stop with all this formality and call me Tom? inspector is such a mouthful."

"Of course. But where are you taking us?"

"To an old army buddy's house. No one knows about him and if the worse did happen, he will be able to protect you better than I could," the inspector said.

"Okay, if you are sure," I said.

"Say, I've been meaning to ask you. Are you any relation to General Rankin, the delta force commandos?" Tom asked.

I take a deep sigh. "Yes, he's my father."

Everyone in the world knows General Rankin. Just mentioning his name brings back memories of his success in the Falklands conflict, being the first team to set foot there after the invasion. The stories make out that he single-handedly captured Port Talbot. That was a long time ago, but army personnel never seem to forget.

"Wow, what a small world. I was sorry about what happened to him," Tom added.

"Why? What were you told? There seem to be lots of conflicting stories," I asked, not giving anything away. It was a line I was used to saying, too often.

"I got told he died while looking for Nazi officers in Austria. Is that true?"

"Yes, Austria, Nazi officers. It was a shame," I said.

"I'm sorry for your loss and the country's loss, too. He was a great leader of men."

"Oh yes, he was. Just not a very good father. He seldom showed up for his kids."

"Unfortunately, that is the army life. The higher your rank, the more time you're away," Said Tom. "Any way, we're almost here. You'll like Doug. He served with your dad, too."

"Oh, that's wonderful," I said.

"I'm sorry about your dad, too. I lost mine when I was young and I know how much it hurts, not being able to say goodbye," said Janie.

I smiled at her, and she smiled back.

We pulled into the driveway of a well maintained, detached Victorian house. Two cars were parked in the driveway. The house seemed to have five or six bedrooms based on its size. The car stopped. A casually dressed man in his sixties greeted us, wearing a tracksuit with white stripes. As Tom opened the driver's door, the man moved towards him.

"Tommy gun," he said as they met and held an embrace.

"It's been too long, Doug," Tom replied.

Janie and I exited the car and stood waiting awkwardly. The inspector saw us and led his friend towards us. He was a big built man that still looked to have kept himself fit. His hair was thinning a little, and he had a few specks of grey.

"Doug, this is Bruce and Janie."

I stepped forward and shook his outstretched hand. Janie did the same.

"Any friend of Tommy is a friend of mine. You are both very welcome here," he said. "Come on, let me introduce you to my wife."

He led us into his house and his wife was waiting in the hallway for us. She struck me as ex-army too. Not sure what it was, but as an army child, you can always tell. She was slim and wore a flowery dress down to her knees, showing off quite muscular legs,

"Hello, hello. Welcome to our humble abode," she said.

"Bruce and Janet, this is my lovely wife, Celine," said Doug.

We both shook her hand.

"And it's Janie," I corrected.

"I am so sorry. I lost a lot of hearing in the war.

"Hey Doug, you'll never guess who this is?" said Tom loudly from behind me, holding my shoulders.

"Go on, tell me. I hate guessing," said Doug.

"This is General Rankins' boy," said Tom loudly.

"Well fuck my boots, you're little Brucey?" he grabbed me and hugged me like I was a family member.

"I served with your dad in the Falklands. He was a sergeant then, bloody good soldier." His smile turned to a frown. "So sorry to hear about his death. Me and the boys were drunk for a week after that one. Not many of us left now. Everyone seems to vanish nowadays. Come on, let's get you settled. Celine?"

His wife showed us to our rooms. Two smallish rooms next to each other and neither one had a double. I'm sure Celine could see the disappointment on our faces.

"I'm joking. This is your room," she said with a big, beaming smile on her face.

That's when I realized our time hiding with Doug and Celine would be filled with fun and pranks.

"Tea's on, so don't be long, you guys," said Celine, heading back down the stairs. "Oh, and your room has an on-suite bathroom, but that door there is another bathroom if you both get cut short at the same time." She pointed to the door at the end of the landing and disappeared down the stairs.

"Bruce!" the inspector called up the stairs. I moved to the top of the stairs and could see him standing at the bottom with a hand on the banister.

"You'll be safe here. Dougie has some tricks ready, just in case. I'll get a couple of officers to grab you a few things from your houses and I'll pop them along tomorrow as soon as I can, ok?" he stated.

"Yes, we'll manage, and thank you Tom," I said.

"Yes, thank you, inspector," Janie called from behind me.

Tom left and Doug closed the front door behind him. Janie and I descended the stairs and met our hosts in the lounge.

"Right, a few ground rules, you two. One, in the event of us being under siege from these mafia shysters, you take Steve McQueen to the power substation, where there is a car primed and ready to go. Just open the gates and off you go. No stopping."

"What the hell is a Steve McQueen?" I asked, and regretted having to ask, scared of what the answer could be.

"I'm glad you asked," he said.

He moved to a bookcase under the stairs and pointed to a book.

"Notice the book. The great escape by Paul Brickhill. It's the little things that bring the greatest of joy."

He touched the book and waited for dramatic effect, before pulling the top of it and tilting it downwards. Clunking and moving sounds filled the air until the bookcase ejected itself from the wall, making me jump unexpectedly. He swung the bookcase away from the wall like a doorway, revealing a dark room or passageway.

"It's an escape tunnel. I built it myself," he said proudly. "It goes down about thirty meters and runs about half a mile under the houses to the electricity power station two streets away."

"Half a mile?" I questioned in shock.

"Yes, that took some digging, I can tell you," he added. "How long was it, Celine?"

"About eighteen months, give or take," she said with a smile.

"My back has never been the same since." He smiled at me.

"You're nuts," I said, almost laughing back at him.

"Yes, but in a Tommy Mallet sort of way. But seriously, if things do get hot, get yourselves down there quick smart. There are torches on the wall. Go past the wine cellar, and past the armoury and turn left. Well, you have to go left. There is no other way, but you get what I mean," he said, pointing into the darkness.

"You have an armoury?" Janie asked in disbelief.

"Yes, help yourselves to anything you want on your way out just in case you have to shoot your way out the other end, but I doubt they know about Steve McQueen. I didn't even get permission to build it, so it's not on any record anywhere," he stated proudly. "The substation isn't even real. We had it put in later just to make sure no one got in at the other end," he added.

"You seem to have thought of everything Doug, I'm impressed," I said.

"Actually, praise where praise is due; it's fucking amazing," said Janie, stepping in for a closer look.

Suddenly, a knock was heard at the front door. Doug pulled Janie back and closed the bookshelf door.

"Don't panic Mr Mannering. That'll be the food," Said Celine.

Looking behind, she ensured everything was normal, then opened the door. A young lad or girl, I couldn't really tell, was standing there in a leather jacket and motorbike helmet with a bag of takeaway containers.

"Delivery for Mrs Willmott?" they said in a deep male voice.

"Thank you darling," Celine said as she took the bag and then closed the door. "Tea's ready," she added, moving to the dining room.

It was a huge feast and I, for one, was grateful for such a big meal. Both Janie and I hadn't eaten since breakfast, and that was a small continental one at that. It was a tourists' Chinese meal. What I mean by that is, it was the basic popular food that every Tom, dick, and Harry gets. We had loads of egg fried rice, sweet and sour chicken balls, special curry and beef and pineapple. All delicious Chinese foods but basic. But then I suppose that our hosts may not have been sure of what we did or didn't like, so this was a safe bet. I enjoyed every mouthful of it.

We ate and joked and talked about Doug and my father on the Falkland Islands. Doug boasted about how my father single-handedly took out a whole machine gun emplacement with nothing but his revolver and his knife, without them even knowing he was there. It sounded fantastic, but I suppose you had to be there to really appreciate it. It was nice to hear people talk about the good in my father, as I had nothing but empty memories of him.

He was never home during his army days and when he did retire; he ran off chasing the Nazi gold in Austria which was the straw that broke the camels' back, for my mother, and she changed all the locks on our house and told him not to come back. I remember they divorced a couple of years later and within a few short years; she died of cervical cancer and left Michael and me to fend for ourselves. We inherited the house, and I invested the money from the sale of it for both of us. He bought his hotel, and I bought my house and converted it into four flats and have been living rent free with a small income from it ever since. That is how I could help out Costanza financially when Michael died.

Suddenly, the television turned itself on and a quiet alarm sounded. The screen exhibited four angles of the house, capturing both the back and front. There were men dressed in black on all sides.

"Shit, already. Get to Steve McQueen now!" he shouted. "Go, go!" he added when we didn't move immediately from the shock.

Janie and I stood from the table and ran to the bookcase. I pulled the book, and the door opened.

"What about you two?" I asked.

He stood behind us, facing the back door with a machine gun in his hands. Where he got that from, I had no idea. Celine appeared with another machine gun and stood facing the front door.

"We'll hold them off as long as we can to give you a chance to escape," Doug said, cocking his gun.

"Don't be stupid. Come with us; both of you," I pleaded.

"Please come with us," Janie cried.

"We got this. Don't worry about us. We've defended worse places than this. We'll be fine."

Had they really? I found it hard to believe that Celine had, but I wasn't going to waste any more time.

"Thank you both," I said as I pushed Janie towards the ladder. "Go," I added.

She descended the ladder, and I quickly followed her.

"Be safe," Celine called out as Doug closed the bookshelf behind me.

When I reached the bottom of the ladder, I could hear gunfire above and hoped that our new friends would be fine, but I honestly didn't think that they would be. I accidentally kicked Janie as I got off the ladder. It was so dark down there.

"Find the torch," I called out to her, not knowing where she was.

Above us, Doug and Celine had 'dug into' their positions and were returning fire. Doug stood by the front door, while Celine occupied the lounge near the bay window. The intruders were on the grounds, hiding behind the two cars in the driveway. Each time one of the intruders showed himself to fire at the house, Doug or Celine would shoot them dead with expert precision. An intruder leapt out from his hiding place behind one of the two cars on the driveway and was about to throw a grenade, but Doug shot him twice, centre mass, and he exploded as soon as he hit the floor. There was a short pause in the fighting, and Doug looked across to Celine.

"No regrets, my love," he said.

"No regrets, my love," she replied.

Suddenly, three men appeared from their hiding places and all three had hand grenades. Two of them were taken out, but the third managed to throw a grenade through the window of the lounge. Celine ran for cover with her husband at the side of the open doorway. Both Celine and Doug were knocked off their feet by the force of the three exploding grenades. One of the outside grenades made Doug's pride and joy, the old Bentley, fly into the street. The intruders took that opportunity to send two more grenades through the open doorway. Doug looked at Celine and they both smiled, knowing what was about to happen.

I felt around in the darkness for the torch. Suddenly, Janie had it in the air and the light was illuminating the darkness. I held on to Janie's free hand and led her in the direction we were instructed. We got as far as the armoury when an almighty explosion happened above us. Dust and small pieces of masonry from the concreted ceiling above us scattered over our heads. The ground beneath us shook like an earthquake.

That was surely the end of our hosts. I decided to bring a gun given the situation above. I chose a semi-automatic; I think it was a Glock and two spare bullet holder things. I have no idea what they were called. I think they called them clips in the movies, but who knew? No time to waste now.

We hurried along the corridor until we reached the ladder up. I went first and Janie followed me. I wanted to make sure all was clear before we climbed out of our hole in the ground.

The old Ford Fiesta was waiting for us with the keys in the ignition, as promised.

"I'll open the doors, and you pull her out so I can close it all up behind us," I instructed Janie.

"I can only drive automatics," she said.

"Ok then, you open the doors and close them behind us," I added.

It started the first time, which surprised me, and I pulled it out of the structure that was supposed to be the substation. Janie quickly closed the door and ran to the gate.

"It's locked," she called out to me.

Fuck, where was the key? I checked the keys in the ignition and there was an extra one. I took the keys out of the ignition and removed the extra key and wound down the window to give it to Janie.

"Here," I called to her. She ran over to the car, took the key, and ran back to the gate. The gate swung open, and I pulled the car through it and waited for it to be closed.

"Don't forget to lock it," I called, out the window.

She did and ran to the passenger door and quickly climbed in. I sped away from the substation and down the street. I could see in the rear-view mirror a huge plume of smoke bellowing upwards a few streets away. What had happened to the house? Did the Willmotts blow it themselves, or did the invaders do it?

"My God! Have you seen it?" she asked in awe.

"Yes. But how the fuck did they find us so quick again? I thought only the inspector knew."

"But would he put his long-term friends at risk by telling them? I don't think he would have," said Janie.

"No, neither do I. He must have told someone, and my money is on his sergeant. What's his name…Wilkinson?" I added.

"Yes! That's the bastard's name," Janie said.

We both thought about it for a while until I noticed that the fuel was almost on empty.

"We need fuel," I said.

"What are we going to do now, Bruce?" she asked.

"I don't know. We'll get some fuel and get as far away from this area as possible. We'll head north. Until we think it's safe."

An Esso garage came into view quite quickly and it had a Tesco's extra attached to it. I pulled into the forecourt and stopped at a pump.

"I'll fill her up and you get us a few supplies, some food and drink. I'll pay for it all when I get there," I told her.

She did as she was instructed and headed to the shop while I filled up the Fiesta. When full, I headed to the shop where Janie was waiting with a basket full of groceries.

"I didn't know how long it has to last, so I got a couple days' worth," she said when she saw me.

"No worries, good idea," I replied.

It cost me seventy-three pounds to get out of there and I decided to use my card. I know they could probably find us by it, but I felt I had no choice.

"You get back in the car. I'm going to draw out as much cash as I can. They can't trace us if we use cash," I told her.

"Let me do the same, the more the merrier by the sounds of it," she added.

We both drew out our maximum limits. She got three hundred, and I got five.

"That should be enough to get us there," I said as we climbed back into the old Ford with our bag of groceries.

"Get us to where?" she asked.

"Well, I've been thinking about it, and the only place I know we will be safe is a long way from here."

"The further, the better, if you ask me," she said. "But where?"

I drove the car off the forecourt and headed for the motorway, which was about six miles from where we were.

"Where?" she repeated.

"We're going to my dad's island," I told her.

"Your dad had an island?" she asked.

"Has, he's not dead," I told her with a smile.

"But you and everyone kept saying he's dead. Even Doug, God rest his soul, said he went to the funeral and everything."

"I went to the funeral as well. It doesn't mean he's dead," I said.

"Hmm, well, usually it does. My dad was definitely dead when we buried him. At least I fucking hope so," she joked.

"I mean, he just wanted everyone to think that he was dead and paid for the funeral himself."

"That's not a normal thing to do. Why would he want to do that?" she asked.

"I don't know. He was a show-off like that. Maybe he wanted to see who loved him or something."

"I take it you two don't get on much?"

"Not much. First I heard, before his fake death, he got back from his treasure hunting in Austria and moved onto an island off the northern coast of Ireland," I said.

"I have been there, but that was a long time ago. He had started to build his communal house in the middle of a lake, but I doubt he ever finished.

I clicked the indicator left, and we pulled onto the M5 and headed north. We needed to get to Manchester then to Dumfries for the ferry across to Ireland.

"Just so you know, it's gonna be at least an eight hours drive before we get to the ferry," I told her. "Shit, have you got photo I.D. on you? A driving license?" I added.

"Yes in the back of my phone, with my bank cards, why?"

"You'll need it to get on the ferry if we haven't got passports," I said.

"You don't need passports for northern Ireland."

"No, but we do for the ferry. Trust me, been there before."

Chapter Four

I trudged through the night, or the rest of it, hungry and exhausted. Janie slept most of the way even though I stopped for coffee and to had a pee twice. I was so tired by the time we reached the ferry port of Cairnryan. I preferred that one to Liverpool as some bastard stole my car from Liverpool last time. But if I had thought about it more, that pokey little Fiesta wasn't my car, and being ninety-nine percent sure that Doug and his wife were dead, I didn't think it mattered much. So, I could have saved myself some time behind the wheel, and anyway, I was taking the car with us this time.

I did, however, think that we were going to set off an alarm or something going through customs, even though we had done nothing wrong. It was like we were fugitives on the run from the law. Janie said that she found it stressful too, but she said she just followed my lead and hoped for the best. I almost shit my pants when I realised I still had the Glock in the car. Luckily, they didn't search the car, but they looked in the boot and checked under the vehicle with a mirror for something. But that turned out to be the requirement for some kind of high alert over something they won't talk about with members of the public. We joked about it on the crossing to Belfast, of how we could be a modern-day Bonnie and Clyde.

It also felt nice having someone to confide in and share inner thoughts with. The cuddling and sex were good too, and all of which I hadn't experienced for a long time. Putting someone else first was something I thought I could never do. I always saw myself as a narcissist and incapable of love, real love, but recent experiences have proven that theory wrong. So, should I believe it was my parents not showing me enough love? Not holding me and cuddling me or whatever, because they didn't. We were not a touchy-feely kind of family. Perhaps they spoke words like 'I love you,' but maybe they never truly believed it in their hearts.

Oh, and there I was on my way to seek refuge with one of them, who has pretended he is dead to the world for whatever reasons he had. Who has hid himself away through most of my childhood and only really trying to get to know me after he died. You know what I mean.

All things aside, he may not have been a brilliant father, but he was an outstanding soldier. Mum showed us, as kids, all the medals for bravery he had won and regaled us with stories of his achievements in the service. If only ten percent of what she told us, as kids, was true, then he was the best option Janie and I had at staying alive, if that was possible. I know that on this island of his; he had a lot of his army buddies living there, too. It must be some sort of retreat for retired service personnel. So, if I remembered that fact correctly, there would be a few soldiers that could also help to protect us. If they were willing and if they could. My God, what was I asking them to do for me, a complete stranger? No, this was a mistake.

"Janie, this is a mistake. I've been thinking of what we will be asking these people to do for us," I told her.

I hadn't realised, because I was so deep in thought, that Janie was hanging her head over the side railings trying not to be sick and I was next to her, rubbing her back. All this must have happened by reflex because it suddenly struck me where we were and what we were doing, and it kind of shocked me. My thoughts clearly distracted me.

"Why didn't you tell me you get seasick? We could have flown if I knew," I told her.

"Didn't know I was. I've never been anywhere before. I could have been sick flying, too," she said. "Come on, distract me. Talk about something, anything. Tell me about your dad."

"Not a lot to tell, really. The army was his life. He was very good at what he did and climbed the ranks quickly. He was the youngest colonel and the youngest general they had ever had. Special forces was his area of expertise. First in to battle, albeit covertly, in through the back door, kill as many as they could to distract the enemy while the full force knocked at their front door. Well, that's how he described it, anyway."

"Doug said he served with him in the Falklands conflict. I remember reading about it or seeing something on the news when it was some sort of anniversary of the war," she said, turning to face me.

She looked a little green under the gills. I chuckled a little and regretted it, but she also laughed so that was ok.

"Can I get you anything to make you feel better?" I asked her.

"No, I'll be fine. How long until we port?" she asked.

"About twenty minutes, miss." A stranger said as he walked past.

"Thank you," I called after him, and he waved his hand in the air.

"I thought I had better tell her. After we port, an hour's drive to Ballycastle is required, followed by a small boat ride to Dad's island. It is only about a six-mile crossing, but it does sometimes get rough in the smaller boat. We can do it tomorrow if you want and stay in Ballycastle overnight, but I'd feel safer the quicker we get to the island. You know how quickly they seem to find us."

I saw the pain in her eyes as she looked at me.

"We should just get it done, or it will spoil two days for me."

"Ada girl," I said. Not sure where those words came from. I held her in my arms and tried to comfort her as best I could. She snuggled in to me and it was so nice to have her there.

A voice instructed passengers to go to their cars but wait for further instructions before starting the engines.

"Shall we?" I asked her.

"No, just a couple more minutes. This is nice," she replied.

I obliged her as it felt good to me too. Soon, we both had to go down to the car. The Fiesta felt cold inside, but I restrained myself from starting the engine to warm it until given permission.

Soon, all the cars gently revved their engines, trying to warm them up, and slowly filtered out of the stern of the ferry. They had always impressed me, these ferries. How did they float with the front and back open for traffic and the sea? Very impressive. Our turn came, and we drove up the short incline and onto terra firma. We drove straight through the customs part and headed for Ballycastle.

"You better now we're on dry land?" I asked her.

"Yes, I am now, and I'm starving," she replied.

"What have we got left to eat?" I asked.

"Some chocolate cookies and…" she rustled into the bag. "No, that's about it," she added.

"Then cookies it is," I said.

"Cookies," she said in a funny voice.

"What was that?" I smiled at her.

"Didn't you ever see that blue monster character, Cookie monster, on Sesame street? I used to love it as a kid."

"Yes, cookie," I said.

During the next half an hour, we entertained ourselves with impressions of the different Sesame Street characters. Mainly the cookie monster, fuelled by every time she asked me if I wanted one and then every time she passed it over to me. We hadn't laughed so much on the journey.

It took us no time at all to reach our next destination. At the ticket office, they informed us we would have to wait two hours for the last ferry of the day. They were expecting severe weather and that we wouldn't be able to return until the morning.

I informed them about our visit to friends and inquired if there was a place to freshen up and grab a bite during the wait.

They pointed us to the automated public toilets on the harborside. Then, we headed to the Promenade café, which overlooks the harbour, and the boats docked there. Considering it was almost twelve o'clock and what I would call dinner time; we expected to see more diners. We chose the best seats by the window to enjoy watching the boats in the harbour as we ate. The waitress appeared at our table and her words made Janie jump.

"What can I get you two lovebirds?" Her inquiry seemed rehearsed and matter of fact. I expect she had said it thousands of times over however many years she had been working there.

"What do you fancy?" I asked Janie, with her head buried in the menu.

"I don't know. What do you recommend?" she asked the waitress.

"If you like fish, then the Pollock is fresh this morning and the chef will pan fry it in a beer and herb marinade and it comes with chunky chips and peas. If you like something else, then his fisherman's pie or his steamed steak and kidney pudding, both served with chips or mash, are a couple of my favourites. But really, everything is wonderful here," she said, with her pen poised above her pad.

"Ooh, I'll have the steak pudding with mash and a little gravy, if possible." I looked across the table at Janie. "Janie?"

"Nothing too heavy for me. I'll have the Pollock please."

We passed the menus to the waitress.

"Thank you," Janie said.

"Will be about ten to fifteen minutes. Do you want something to drink?" she asked.

"Ooh, I'd love a strong coffee?" I asked her, and she scribbled it on her pad.

"Yes, me too," said Janie.

We both looked out the window, lost in our own thoughts. The waitress returned with our coffees after a couple of minutes.

"Bruce, do you think they'll find us?" Janie asked.

"Honestly, yes, I expect so. I doubt it will happen soon, as nobody knows our location. Even dad doesn't know we're coming," I assured her.

"But they always seem to find us. I'm scared."

I held her hands across the table and tried to reassure her.

"My father is an outstanding soldier. A leader of men in the elite world of special forces. That makes him someone special. He has surrounded himself with like-minded friends from his army days and truth be told, I expect most of them will be ex-special forces or something similar. My dad always plans ahead and has a contingency plan for situations like this."

I, of course, didn't believe a word of it. From my last visit, around six years ago, I recall seeing many elderly individuals, none of whom seemed fit for special forces. But I would not tell Janie that. It would only worry her. He did, however, start building his castle, as he called it. A sanctuary for everyone on the island during hurricanes and other dangers. I secretly hoped he had finished his project by now, because somehow we may need it; sooner than he thinks.

I know he wasn't the kind of man to shy away from danger and I know he would not turn us away, but everything else might just be asking too much. Plus, we were all six years older. Especially my dad and all the geriatrics I saw last time I was there.

Our food arrived, and it was delicious. The waitress wasn't lying when she said everything tasted good. It was the best steak pie I have ever eaten. Janie loved the Pollock, too. We left the café an hour later, fed and watered and ready for the last leg of our journey. We emptied the car; not that we had much to carry. A bag with a couple pairs of jeans and a couple of tee shirts we bought on the road. We were going to need some more clothes and some warmer ones. It felt ominously cold, and it dug deep into me. It was a lot colder than yesterday. We were a lot farther north than we were yesterday. The island was only five miles north of Ballycastle and only twelve miles south of the Mull of Kintyre on the coast of Scotland. That's probably why it was so cold.

We headed to the harbour where the 'Spirit of Rathlin', a small ferry, was arriving. We returned to the ticket office and paid eight pounds each for a single journey and climbed aboard and sat down on the lower deck inside, where I hoped it would be warmer.

Janie didn't seem too excited for another sea crossing, and I noticed she had a bag in her hand this time.

"It will be as smooth as silk crossing the sound," I assured her.

"I know, but I was a girl guide and I'm just being prepared," she said with a chuckle.

I, for one, had mixed feelings. It's not about the crossing, it's about reuniting with my father after so long. We didn't part on very good terms last time because I was angry at him for not attending Mum's funeral. I know he was dead, technically, but he could have watched it from a distance or something. Despite the divorce, he must have once loved her and should have been there for the boys. I'm afraid I was very vocal about it the last time we met, and it had left a sour taste in my mouth ever since. I shouldn't have expected anything else from him, to be honest. He was absent from his boys when needed, even during their marriage. So why expect him to be there for an ex-wife?

We hadn't seen him at my graduation, Michael's marriage to Costanza, and then mum's funeral. Even Michael's funeral, come to think of it. I was too soft and should have cut ties with him years ago, back when we parted on bad terms. But I needed him more than ever, hoping for his understanding and forgiveness.

I had lied to Janie; the crossing was not what you'd call as smooth as silk. Because of the storm, the ferry jolted and plunged constantly. Janie had to use her bag, and as we had just eaten; it was not much fun for her. Thankfully, it was only an hour crossing. It should have been forty minutes, but with the sea being so choppy, the land didn't come soon enough, for Janie.

"Welcome to Dad's island," I said as we stepped onto the concrete jetty.

Well, she didn't look impressed. I thought she was going to punch me when I said we still had an hour's walk to Dad's. I had forgotten to mention that bit.

We walked past the various houses and holiday accommodations, including the Manor house hotel. I remember a road linking the houses and the pub, taking us to where Dad started building his 'castle'.

Rathlin Island has a rich history. It was the site of the first Viking raid in Ireland. The pillaging of its church and the burning of houses took place in 795. In 1306, Robert the Bruce took refuge on the island and stayed in Rathlin Castle and eventually became king of Scotland from 1306 to 1329. He led the Scottish during its first war of independence from the English.

Guglielmo Marconi made the first wireless telegraphy transmission from East lighthouse on the island to Ballycastle on 6th July 1898.

German U-boats torpedoed various ships from 1917 to 1918, and these ships sought refuge in Church Bay harbour before sinking offshore. Among them were HMS Drake and the RMS Andania, to name a couple.

Now tourism plays a major part in the island's economy with a short holiday season because of being so far north.

The storm was getting closer, and the rain had started to fall. Only lightly in the wind, but we got soaked anyway. As we looked up, black clouds gathered, promising a wild night.

Dad lived on the edge of Ushet lake, the island's southernmost lake. It was a four-mile walk, with some steep hills to climb. Luckily, it was a tarmac road all the way. Despite our timely arrival, exhaustion overwhelmed us. Because of our improper clothing for the weather, both Janie and I ended up freezing and soaking wet by the time we caught sight of the lake.

What I witnessed left me breathless. Dad had finished his castle. In the middle of the lake there stood a huge, stone walled castle. It must have been thirty feet high and a couple of hundred feet square. Each corner had a round tower. The castle itself had a five- or six-feet high curtain wall around it and a lush green lawn between it and the castle walls. The gatehouse stood taller than the walls with a massive metal drawbridge blocking the only visible entrance.

This was excessive, dad. It must have cost a fortune. How did he get permission for this eyesore? Lots of questions after we work out how to gain entry.

"That's some ego your father has, Bruce," Janie said with a smile.

"You said it Janie," I replied.

The tarmac road led to the lake's edge, resembling a moat for the castle. A speaker with two buttons stood on a nearby stand. One black, one red, but otherwise identical. Dad always joked with us kids about never pushing a red button. Red buttons are danger, he used to say, when he was there, of course. Ok, I remembered what he told me, so I pushed the black button, and we waited for a reply.

"Who goes there?" came an old man's voice on the speaker.

"Is the general coming out to play?" I replied. That's what we said when we knocked on the parent's door, us two boys. Back then, it was colonel or captain or whatever rank he was.

"Bruce, is that you?" my father's voice asked.

"Yes, Dad, and we're cold and wet too. Please let us in before this storm hits."

The metal drawbridge creaked and lowered itself and landed too quickly, with a thud, on the bank in front of us. Standing inside was my father, and three other men dressed in army gear holding what looked like assault rifles. The castle guard, I had thought to myself. He beckoned us in under the shelter from the rain. I helped Janie over the metal drawbridge, and I breathed an enormous sigh of relief as we stepped into the shelter of the barbican.

He appeared even younger, if that was possible. His alternative lifestyle certainly agreed with him. He had lost a little more hair, but it had not yet changed colour. Despite being technically dead and almost seventy, he looked good, probably because he dyed his hair.

"Son, it's so good to see you again. If you had said you were coming, I would have sent the chopper. But don't worry, you are here now. Come in, come in. Let's get you somewhere warm and out of those wet clothes," he said, unusually welcoming.

"Dad, this is Janie and Janie, this is my father, General Rankin," I told her.

"Oh God, call me Monty, lovely to meet you." They shook hands. "Come on in. Let's get you warm by the fire," he said, taking Janie by her waist and leading her into a doorway on the left in the Barbican.

I heard the drawbridge close with a loud metal thud as we made our way into the opulent surroundings. It looked like it was royal accommodation. Everything was marble floored and plush thick rugs on top, with tapestry and oil paintings on the walls. L.E.D. bulbs, designed to look like candles, hung from the walls, evoking the era when castles were essential and not just a symbol of affluence. He led us to a doorway to a lounge area. There were thirty comfy armchairs in the room, giving it a huge look. Some of them occupied by newspaper reading and sleeping old folk. The fireplace was at least six feet high and eight feet across. Dad pulled a couple of armchairs closer to the fire and held the back of one, like a true gentleman, while Janie sat in it.

It was so welcoming; The stress of the last couple of days melted away into the warmth like a candle. Our clothes would be dry in no time. I needed to tell dad what was going on, but he vanished, and I was not sure where he had gone. He soon reappeared with a small table with a decanter of whiskey and a couple of glasses on it. He poured some whiskey into the two tumblers and offered them to Janie and me.

"I won't take no for an answer," he said. "You must be cold, but this will warm you."

We didn't refuse; he was right. It was the smoothest whiskey I had ever tasted and usually, that meant it was expensive. Where did all this opulence come from? I needed answers, but it was comfy where I was for now. The questions could wait. Dad pulled another armchair by us and slightly facing us.

"How have you been, Bruce? Honestly, I never expected to see you again after our last encounter."

"I'm sorry we left it like that, dad, but you can be overbearing and selfish," I said, determined to say it as I saw it.

"A bit. I was unbearable. You are absolutely right, and I can explain all of it to you later when you are back to your normal selves. Janie, if you want some clean clothes, I'm sure we can find some for you. If not, we'll send out for some," he said.

"Thank you. I will need something. These are not drying well," she replied.

"And did you say chopper just now, as in helicopter?" I asked him.

"Yes. Living here requires a chopper, as there are no trains or buses, and many residents cannot manage the walk you just completed. They'd break a hip. Wouldn't you Margot?"

The old lady in the chair nearest to Janie opened her eyes.

"Not my new titanium ones I wouldn't, Monty." She laughed and so did Dad.

"She was struggling, bless her, so we all chipped in and made her bionic, as she calls it. Gave her a completely new lease on life," he added.

"Dad, everywhere I look, there is wealth and helicopters and titanium hips. Since the state pension doesn't cover everything, where is the money coming from? This castle must have cost millions to build," I asked him.

"Almost seventy million, but who's counting? We can talk later when you're both settled. We eat at around seven o'clock. I'll give you the guided tour in the morning," Dad said.

"Dad, there's something important you should know."

"I thought there must be, but here you are safe and will be warm and fed in no time. Then we can talk about everything, answer all our questions," he said.

"I need the talk tonight dad, it is important."

"After tea, we'll head to the den for a conversation over a few drams. You get warm and take care of Janie," he added.

I have never seen him so caring and, well, nice. At least from the offset, he seems to have become a changed man. I was curious about the source of this wealth, but that was just the accountant in me. We sat and warmed ourselves in front of the fire for ages. Whenever it seemed to die, someone added another log. I was so tired; I hadn't slept in two days and must have fallen straight to sleep in the comfy armchair.

The old lady, Margot, woke me. "Come on Bruce, dinner will be ready soon," she said, shaking my arm.

Janie had clearly already woken, as if she had gone to sleep and was standing arm in arm with Margot. I stood and took the other arm. Janie and I led Margot to the dining area, following her instructions. Inside the dining area was an enormous table. Roughly fifty feet long, with approximately the same number of chairs encircling it. On the table were massive silver platters of fruit and glass goblets with eight or ten glass decanters of white and red wine, water, and some orange juice.

Pensioners quickly filled the chairs, and they all recognized and greeted each other as they sat. The room soon filled with a polite humdrum of voices. Two older gentlemen stood by the side of where Janie and I were sitting.

"I think we are in their seats," said Janie.

"Are you Monty's boy, Brian?" one of the old gents said.

"Yes, and it's Bruce," I replied.

"You'll sit at the Captain's table in the other room,"

the other elderly man affirmed, "Yes, that's correct. The Captain's table," he added.

We both stood, and I took Janie's hand and led her to the doorway. We could hear sniggering behind us. The two men sat in our seats, laughing with others. I ignored them but couldn't help but sense that we had fallen victim to a prank or something. I opened the door to the kitchen and there was no captain's table. The laughing became a roar behind us. Those old rogues had tricked us to get our seats. Their bodies may look old, but their minds were as sharp as a tack. I looked into the kitchen again.

"Oh, shit, can someone give me a hand, quick we need to stand her up," I said, letting go of Janie's hand.

The chef looked at me in wonder, so I gave her a wink and she understood. Three elderly men bolted from the table and passed by me in the doorway. I grabbed Janie's hand and quickly pulled her back to the table, and we sat down to the roar of the others. Upon seeing nothing amiss in the kitchen, the three rescuers smiled and conceded to the roaring of the others. They pulled another table from the wall and set it at the end of the long one. After finding some chairs, we all laughed together.

Soon the kitchen door flung open, and the chef called out. "Ready guys," she called.

Four men left their seats and returned from the kitchen with food. There were several large bowls carried in and placed strategically on the table. The men carried in four platters of sausages and strategically placed them at points along the table. Then came the large glass jugs of baked beans. We were having bangers and mash for tea. I somehow expected more, like a roast or something fit for a banquet. Yet, considering the circumstances, practicality was required because of the large number of mouths to feed. My father was nowhere to be found, so I had to inquire.

"Is the general joining us?"

"No lad, he never eats with us. He and the two colonels eat at the Captain's table." I wasn't sure who said that, as no one was looking directly at me.

"I'm not falling for that one again," I said with a smile.

Anyway, I was starving and was not going anywhere until after I had eaten. The old man regaling her with stories of his past deeds engrossed Janie. He was obviously trying to chat her up. From time to time, she would gaze and smile at me while I smiled back at her. I almost choked on my food when she dropped her hand into my lap and gave it a squeeze. She couldn't help but find it hilarious but pretended the old man's story caused her laughter. I received a pat on the back from the elderly gentleman beside me, urging me to eat at a slower pace.

After the meal, they showed us to our room for the night. Janie requested that I not wake her when I returned from the den, as she wanted to sleep. I had almost forgotten about the den. Yes, I wanted to let dad know what had happened to us so that he could at least prepare.

Chapter Five

I tucked Janie into the huge four-poster bed draped with lace or a cotton material that made it resemble something from a fairytale. Janie said she felt like a princess. I kissed her goodnight and promised her I would come back later. Her worry persisted from the past few days. But then, who can blame her? The minute we seemed to relax, so trouble would show up.

Leaving her and the cuddles behind was hard, but Dad had to be informed. I left silently and searched for the stairs we used. There were old people everywhere. Well, I say old, that was a little unfair. They were definitely older than me. Their ages ranged from fifty plus to I would say ninety, but they all had one thing in common; they were all spritely and youthful. Did dad discover a fountain of youth or did this environment truly benefit older generations? Some of them effortlessly bounded up the stairs, putting me to shame. I had to look twice in wonder as I gingerly descended on them.

Despite the lift, everyone opted for the stairs. When I was here before, the men unloading foundation stones astounded me. I envied them back then, but discovering that I still do, six years later, was honestly unsettling.

I had to ask a couple of times for directions to the den. If only Dad had mentioned the dungeon, I could've found it on my own.

"Ah, Bruce, there you are. Come in, let me show you round the place," Dad said proudly.

The room resembled a command centre rather than a den. My idea of a den includes a pool table, a dartboard, and a bar. From here, we can oversee the entire island and observe anything of interest. But this was breathtaking. There were three large L.E.D. TV screens with picture in picture. They divided each screen into twelve unique pictures. It was a camera system; I had seen similar in the security office at the university I went to. There were two men or security I assumed monitoring the screens.

"From here, we can see the entire island and monitor anything we desire," said Dad.

"Isn't that an invasion of privacy?" I asked.

"It's my island. I'll do what I want?" he added.

Dad, Rathlin Island has belonged to the Irish for a while now.

"Uh, no. We own everything south from Mill bay," one guard said.

"Now, Freddy, don't give out all our secrets," said Dad.

"You own… you bought half the island? Dad, where's all this money coming from?" I asked, a little concerned.

"Oh, come on, I'll show you," he said.

I thought he would show me precious gems on the rock walls, or something similar. I never expected what would come next. He led me down a rock-walled corridor where there were four, no five iron cell doors.

"Open three Freddy," Dad shouted back.

There was a loud clunk, and the door swung an inch on its hinges. He pulled the door wide, and we entered. We found two pallets stacked with covered items inside. He grabbed a corner of one tarpaulin and pulled. The air filled with dust, and it took me a couple of seconds to fully grasp what I was seeing.

"What…, where….?" was all I could muster.

Before me was a pallet stacked with gold bars. The gold bars bore the swastika in the talons of an eagle with the words 'Deutsche Reichsbank' imprinted below.

"You found the Nazi gold?" I asked.

"Yes, indeed, we found it in a bunker in the Swiss Alps, along with hundreds of priceless artefacts and paintings and stuff we never knew existed. We struck a deal with the German government to return all the artifacts for a substantial reward, and this is what you're seeing."

"How much is here?" I had to know. Never had I witnessed such an abundance of gold in person.

"Oh, last count was a couple billion, give or take. The value is always changing. We promised the German government that we would not sell to anyone else but them and only one hundred bars a year, as they don't want to flood the gold market and deflate the price of their own reserves."

"It's amazing, but those artifacts didn't belong to the Germans. They stole them during the war. They belonged to the Jews and the other European countries they invaded," I stated.

"Agreed. The German people can make amends by promptly returning the discovered artefacts in the Swiss Alps."

"But why not the gold, too?"

"It's only five percent of the total. Our finder's fee. All legit and above board. But you can see why we needed strong defences to protect this from anyone who wants to steal it from us," he said, covering the gold back up. "Anyway, what's been going on with you? I see you finally got a girlfriend," he added.

"My God, dad, let me catch my breath. This is fantastic. And you shared it with all your army buddies?" I asked.

"Together, we spent three years searching for it. We worked for an equal share, but when we discovered its size and the difficulty of secrecy, we devised this plan. Buy an island and build a castle rest home. It's a perfect idea. Now that everyone has moved in, we even have our own personal garrison to protect it. Nobody wants for anything. We buy in bulk, so no worries about the cost of new Titanium hips or that wonder drug to cure a disease that the national health system couldn't afford. We've never had it so good."

"Dad, I'm at a loss for words. Everyone, including mother thought you were going crazy. Everyone, including mother, never expected that you would actually find it."

"But why fake your death? That bit I don't understand?" I asked.

"It was decided to keep it quiet, considering the commotion I caused while looking for it. It worked. People stopped looking for us after a while. Bigger stories became the news and we all just disappeared onto our island."

He led me back to the control centre and touched Freddy on his shoulder.

"Close three Freddy."

"Everyone here has work to do. We are totally off grid and self-reliant. We take care of the locals, too. The ones who also live on the other part of the island. We've built their new tourist centre and rebuilt their docks to accommodate the new ferry. In fact, the locals love us. We have our own mini-Olympics every year, where they pit their best against our residents. It attracts a lot of tourists every year. But we may stop it soon as the B.B.C. has sniffed around the games looking for a story.”

“Seeing these residents, I thought you found a fountain of youth. I almost expected to find them skinny-dipping in the moat at midnight,” I added.

“I suppose, in a way, we have. All individuals here have the freedom to do as they please. We have a strict fitness regime that everyone must attend to the best of their ability. But, definitely no swimming in the moat. It’s a fresh-water lake and we have a piranha breeding schedule. We have a great program for hobbies and pastimes. We’ve got a gardening club, knitting club, birdwatching club, marine biology club. Everyone is happy,” he said.

“I’m proud of what you’ve accomplished.”

“Thank you son, we are proud of it too,” he said.

“It makes what I’m about to say a little harder,” I added. “Can we go somewhere private and talk, please?” I asked him.

“We have no secrets and no loose lips here, son, one of our rules of residence,” he said.

"Ok, well…" I stammered.

"Come on, son, out with it."

"We came here because we are being hunted by a drugs lord. I saw him kill my boss, and he had tried to get us again at our homes, and we went to a safe house. Actually, you knew him. He was a friend of the detective inspector and apparently you served together with him in the Falkland's conflict. Doug Willmott and his wife Celine."

"Ah yes Dougie. He didn't want to join us on our expedition and so we had to block him out of everything. How is Dougie?" he asked.

"I'm sorry to say that the drug lord found us there, too. Doug and his wife were killed, making sure that we escaped," I said solemnly.

"Ah, damn it, he was a fine soldier and a great man. We will light candles for them at remembrance."

"I think he found us because of the police. They must have a mole or someone working for the gang," I added.

"What is this kingpin's name? Do you know?" he asked.

"Marco Dellucci. Based in Bristol."

"Freddy, find out what you can about this Marco Dellucci and find his whereabouts for me. Let me know the moment you do," said the general.

"Yes sir," said Freddie.

"Do you believe he will come here?" said Dad.

"There will be no court case if he gets rid of the witness," I added.

"No, of course not. That's how his type gets away with things," Dad said. "Ok, I'll call a special meeting tomorrow and we can all discuss what to do. Get a good night's sleep until then. You look exhausted, son."

He wasn't wrong. Apart from my nap in the chair in front of the fire, I hadn't slept for two days.

"Yes, I'm going now, and thanks dad for not chucking us out," I said.

"Son, we have been training for stuff like this all our lives. It would be a big mistake for Marco to come here looking for you."

Freddy and the other man laughed along with him. Clearly, they were not worried either. I wish I had their confidence.

"Get some sleep. Breakfast is about seven o'clock. We'll have a meeting after that, and we will all decide what to do next," he stated calmly.

"Ok, night all," I said, heading for the stone stairs.

This place was quite a piece of engineering if you inspected it. The den and stairs appeared carved from solid rock. But that can't be, as they constructed the castle in the middle of the lake. I pondered many things on my way back to the bedroom, back to Janie. Exhausted, I felt safe for the first time in days. I stressed a little over the fact that I would have to testify against this Marco to stop him and his kind from believing they were above the law. I must contact the inspector to confirm my existence and willingness to testify.

The bedroom was cold when I got back to Janie. The fire had almost burnt out. I dropped my clothes on the chair in front of the slit for a window and rushed to get into bed next to her. I hoped she was warm so that I could snuggle in, but thought no, I best let her sleep. My cold body next to hers would surely wake her. The bedding was fresh and warm, and I must have fallen asleep in no time.

Chapter Six

Janie woke me in the morning, rubbing my chest, playing with the hairs on it.

"Morning sleepy head," she whispered.

I shook off the last of sleep and nestled next to her.

"Morning princess," I replied.

"She laughed. I felt like a princess in this bed. It's magnificent, isn't it?" she replied.

"What time is it?" I asked her.

"A little after seven, I think."

"Quick, get dressed. Breakfast is at seven, followed by a meeting about Marco and what to do next. It's crucial that we attend."

We both braved the cold and clambered for our clothes and changed as fast as possible. I was ready first, but men usually are. Less to dress. She moved to the mirror and looked at her hair.

"Princess, you look beautiful to me. Everyone else couldn't take their eyes off you all night. So don't worry. Come on."

"Without make-up or a hairbrush, you'll see the real me today."

"Wouldn't want you any other way, princess."

I opened the door for her and curtsied. She waved regally, and we laughed as we walked to the dining room. They left two seats empty for us, so there was no need to fight for them. Most of the residents were already eating and chatting. The table had bowls of oats and cornflakes, along with platters of bacon, eggs, and sausages. That's what I wanted and reached for some.

"What do you want, princess?" I asked Janie.

"Hmm, yes, I'll eat some of that. Is there any coffee? I don't function without my coffee on a morning."

"Your wish is my command, your highness," said the old guy next to her. He stood and fetched the coffeepot that was out of range of his arms. He poured her a mug full. "I'm Henry," he added.

"Thank you, Henry. I'm Janie, and this is my boyfriend, Bruce," she said.

"Oh, that was subtle Janie," I whispered to her.

She smiled. "I don't want him getting the wrong idea."

"He's seventy," I whispered.

"With great hearing and I bet I could run circles around you too," said a smiling Henry, passing a jug of milk to Janie.

I think I blushed. Janie laughed.

"One of the residents' rules is, 'everyone treats everyone equally and with respect'. Another is, 'no man will touch another man's woman'," he added. "So, she's safe, Bruce, and lovely to meet you both."

"I'm sorry, Henry…" I started, but Henry spoke over me.

"Here is not like the outside world. I fully understand," he added.

"Thank you, Henry," I said.

"And thank you for the coffee," Janie said.

"What is your role around here, Henry?" I asked.

"He's retired Bruce," Janie interjected.

"No, we all earn our keep around here," he replied. "I run around keeping all the fires fed," he added.

"I've seen them. Quite impressive," I said.

I filled Janie's plate with bacon, eggs, sausages, and a few beans and did the same to mine. Not the best I've eaten, a little too greasy for my taste. But I enjoyed it. Dad appeared from the kitchen. He clapped his hands to get everyone's attention; the room fell silent.

"People! I'm calling an extraordinary meeting of council. My Bruce here has come to us for help. Let's discuss the problem and its resolution. So, I suggest we finish breakfast and shower or whatever and meet back here at zero nine hundred hours. Communications and services, please go to your posts and carry on as normal. The colonels will talk with you individually after and let you cast your votes. Thank you all," he stated.

A quiet humdrum of voices filled the room. Everyone stared at Janie and me, curious about the situation. And rightly so. I was going to throw a spanner in the works and upset the normal status quo here at the castle.

A voting system sounds good, but why would strangers want to help me? I felt in limbo and by Janie's face; she did too. I had told her dad would help with the Marco situation. Now it looked like they had to vote on it. I didn't keep my promise to her, despite her leaving everything behind in Bristol.

Now the food didn't taste as good, and the castle didn't feel as welcoming as it did ten minutes ago. Janie wasn't happy and ignored the conversations from the man sat next to her.

"It'll be fine, don't worry," I told her.

I'm not sure she believed me, but then, I didn't believe it either. While people scattered to their accommodations for various post-breakfast activities, they took the plates and remaining food to the kitchen. Janie and I sauntered away, back to our room. I needed a shower and Janie said she wanted one yesterday, but she was too tired. It was a big shower, and I almost expected Janie to join me for a rubdown, but she sat on the bed deep in her own thoughts. I undressed and opted for a shower, anyway.

"Hey," I called out to her from the shower. "Janie?" and again.

Her head popped around the corner of the bathroom and she suddenly smiled when she understood why I was calling her, then promptly disappeared again. Then she reappeared in all her glory, naked as the day she was born. I was such a lucky man. She was beautiful; dressed or undressed. She entered the cubicle with me and shared the shower with me. I moved aside so that she could get wet and warm from the water jets. We washed each other thoroughly, then dried each other. We wanted to rush straight into bed, but the meeting couldn't start without us, and we certainly shouldn't miss it. So, we hurriedly changed into our clothes in our cold bedroom. The fire was out, and it was cold. I was not sure if we keep it going all night or if someone lights it daily. There was no more kindling wood or logs that I could see. So I don't think we could have kept it going, even if we wanted to.

After getting dressed, we settled on the bed, and Janie clung to my arm, resting her head on my shoulder.

"What are we going to do if they vote against helping us?" she asked.

"I don't know."

It was all I could tell her. I did not know what we would do next. I hadn't thought past getting here and assumed dad would protect us. I looked at the clock on the wall and it was almost twenty-five minutes past eight.

"Let's be brave and face it together."

I stood, raising Janie at the same time. She didn't release my arm until we arrived at the dining area and took our seats. Once we were seated, she held onto my arm again. The chairs were filled with people, and we could hear the usual buzz of voices. Dad appeared and everybody stood and saluted at him. Two others stood beside him, and I assumed they were the colonels we heard about yesterday.

"At ease," he said.

Everyone sat and was silent, then the general continued.

"I call to order this extraordinary meeting of the council to deliberate on the immediate action required to help my son Bruce and his lady Janie. They have a particular problem that I best let him tell you about. Bruce?"

Talk about being thrown in the deep end or thrown to the lions. I stood and Janie took my hand and held on tight to it.

"Well, first of all, thank you all for receiving us and making us feel welcome here. After the last couple of days that we have had, it is most appreciated," I said, as confidently as I could. After all, I was a general's son and didn't want to embarrass him by stammering my way through.

"Janie and I work at an accounting firm in Bristol. On Saturday, some men visited our office and met with our boss, Michael Hamilton II. One man, who we have later found out to be a drugs lord called Marco Dellucci, shot him point blank and killed him. We hid, and he didn't know we saw. He might've killed us, there and then."

There were a few gasps and inaudible mumblings around the room.

"We called the police, and they took statements, etcetera, then we headed back to our homes, well Janie's home first and the front door was already open. We didn't take any chances and drove past, assuming it was the mobsters. To stay safe, we didn't bother going to mine. We disappeared and went to Bath and stayed at a hotel overnight. In the morning I called the detective inspector on the case, and we agreed to meet."

I looked at Janie and she gripped my hand and smiled at me. It gave me some more confidence.

"The inspector took us to what he called a safe house. It was the home of one of yours, Doug Willmott."

A few voices acknowledged the name.

"He and his wife, Celine, made us welcome, but within an hour or two, the house was under siege, and we barely got away before the entire house exploded. Regrettably, I believe Doug and his wife perished because of the gunfire prior to the explosion. If it wasn't for their heroic actions, we would not be here today, and I am so sorry for your loss."

Unbelievably, the room stood and bowed their heads. I didn't want to say anything further until they stopped. A couple of minutes passed, and they sat back down. I paused longer.

"Continue Bruce," my father instructed.

"Well, from there, we travelled through the night and came here. We had nowhere else to go. I discovered the castle and all of you upon arrival. I hope you vote to assist us. Without your support, we are uncertain of our next steps. Thank you for your attention."

I don't know why I added that last bit, but I thought it might help. Noise in the room grew to a loud muttering as they discussed things with the person next to them. The colonel to dad's right stamped his feet and shouted for quiet. The room fell silent, and the colonel continued.

"The question to be answered today is, do we allow the general's son and his girl to stay, and that will mean possibly taking on a heavily armed force of civilians? This could mean engaging violently with them and may even result in some deaths on our own side."

The room burst into laughter. My God, were they taking this seriously? Was this just a joke to them? The laughter yielded, and the room fell quiet as their general motion for quiet with his hands.

"I think we had them at 'armed civilians', sir," said the colonel.

"Troops listen, we have practiced for a day like this. We have rehearsed all scenarios when storming the castle. What this civilian force will not expect is us. We may be a little past our prime, but we were the best of the best. Remember that when you cast your votes."

All the people cheered excitedly. The second colonel, to dad's left, turned and collected a ballot box from against the wall and steadied it on the dining table, along with a stack of what I assumed were ballot papers. The elderly force voted. Father approached Janie and me.

"This may seem like nonsense to you, but we run this place with a democratic hierarchy. The democracy decides; I execute them, army-style. It has served us well over the last few years," he stated.

"But, sir, forgive me…"

The general interrupted her.

"Call me Monty," he said.

"Monty, as I look around, all I see are old people who should enjoy this fantastic retirement you have all created here. Not being at war and possibly getting killed," she said.

"Young lady, let me tell you something about this load of old geriatrics," started the general.

"Steady on, general, speak for yourself," came a voice from behind us.

The general smiled. "Amongst this lot, we have demolitions experts, snipers, special forces from every conceivable regiment. The S.A.S., Delta Force warriors, Commandos. These men and women before you were some of the most feared and most called upon troops in the army, navy, and air force. Some things you never forget, especially when you practice and keep your skills honed well into your old age," he said proudly.

"Come on, let me show you something," he added.

He led us down the stairs to the den or control room.

"Freddy, call up some of the shooting practices we've had. Don't choose the best, just as they come," the general instructed.

Freddy pressed a few buttons on his console. And firing targets appeared on the screens. The first one had three bullseye, two just outside.

"Who is that?" the general asked.

"That's Gordon's sir," Freddy replied.

"Really?" the general asked, surprised. "Well, this is from Gordon. He's eighty-three, I believe," he added.

The following targets, explained as the work of an unlikely suspect, were executed with similar precision.

"Ok, I get it, but fitness has always played a major part in warfare. What about that?" I questioned him.

"Freddy, do we have any footage from the recent ropework?" he asked.

"Yes, sir," replied Freddy, pressing buttons on the keyboard.

Video footage of soldiers abseiling down the castle towers and re climbing back up dominated the screen.

"Who is that Freddy? Do we know?" Dad asked.

"That will be Margaret and Daniel, sir," said Freddy.

It looked impressive, and I certainly couldn't do it.

"Margaret is seventy-three and Daniel is older." The general relished.

"Okay, okay, we get it. Bloody impressive, in fact," I agreed.

"Look! In the forces, you are only as strong as your weakest link. We won't ask a sniper to climb up and down walls before having to shoot. Nor would we ask one of our amputees to run around with a bayonet. Each of us has a specialty that we have kept up with over the years. We have not experienced dementia here, as we keep our minds sharp like combat knives by rehearsing all the things that kept us alive and active in younger years. Sure, we will not break any records, but I dare any equal numbered force to come against mine and not come off worse."

He obviously took great pride in his troops, but because they were also his friends and close acquaintances, his judgment may have been clouded. But I agree, they looked impressive. I only hoped that they would vote in our favour.

"Well, *if* the vote goes our way, I will feel safe, whatever happens," Janie threw in.

"If! If! My God, the vote is just because that's how we do things. These guys would relish the opportunity to put into reality all the practicing and rehearsing we have done over the years. Even if the rehearsals were to stop people from stealing our piggy bank, this is no different," the general stated proudly.

Piggy bank? Did he mean the pallets full of billions of pounds worth of gold bars in the cell next door? That brought a smile to my face.

"What are you smiling about?" asked Janie.

"May I show her dad?" I asked.

He tutted. "Freddy open three."

I took Janie to the gold and watched her face when she saw how much was under the cover.

"This is what he's calling the piggy bank," I said.

Her mouth was wide open. She reached out a hand and picked up one bar.

"It's real," she said, looking at the gold bar in her hand, feeling the weight of it.

"And it's all legit, too. A couple billion pounds worth, give or take," I said, smiling at her.

She looked at me, smiling, with her mouth still agape.

"Yes, I know, right?" I added.

I helped her to replace the gold bar and threw the tarpaulin back over it.

"That's the reason he built the castle to protect his piggy bank. Well, their piggy bank. They all have an equal share of it," I added.

"Close three Freddy," I called. Locks clunked as the door swung closed.

We headed back to the control room, just as the other operator spoke.

"Sir, I have just run facial rec. on two of the men who just got off the ferry from Bally. They both have long criminal records and are ex-forces, believed to be mercenaries for hire."

"What could two mercs possibly want on this island?" the general asked him.

"Sir, they both have links to Bristol and drugs," the operator continued.

"Fuck me. You said they were good. But that was fast. You only arrived yesterday," said the general. "Ok Freddy, get the colonels to meet us here asap."

"They could have traced the car we used. We left it in Ballycastle," I said to him.

"Rookie mistake, but no matter. We'll sort it," Dad said.

"You mean kill them?" asked Janie.

"God, no! We'll throw them in Bruce's cave and let the tide do it," he stated.

"You have a cave named after you?" she asked me.

"Do I?" I asked my dad.

"No, no. It's been called that since Robert the Bruce sought refuge there long ago. We are only twelve miles off the coast of Scotland here," he said. "There's a derelict castle here too, called Bruce's castle, and that's named after the same chap too, sorry."

The colonels entered the control room.

"Gentlemen, we have two mercs just got off the Bally ferry. We believe they are a scouting party for the Dellucci mob. See, they don't find their way here and deposit them in Bruce's cave for interrogation. Set a guard and I'll be along shortly," the general instructed.

"Yes, sir," they said in unison and climbed the stairs.

"Monitor them Freddy, and let the colonels know if anything changes," Dad said.

"Yes, sir," said Freddy.

"Come on," Dad said. "Let's see how many votes you got. Although if those two are who we think they are, the vote is redundant."

"I'm sorry, dad," I said to him.

"Don't be. Like you said, where else could you go? What else could you do? I'm just glad you still thought you could come to me after the way things got last time we met," said Dad.

"Gone and forgotten, as far as I'm concerned," I replied.

"Same here, son. Clean slate?" he asked.

"Clean slate and thanks again for us both," I said.

The general stopped, took a firm hold of me, and we held each other for a few seconds. It almost brought a tear to my eyes. It had been a long time since we had even shaken hands. Maybe he had really changed for the better. Then we patted each other's backs and continued.

"Yes, thank you Monty. Sorry to be a pain," said Janie.

"A pain? Pain is for wimps. You won't find any wimps here," he said with a smile.

Upstairs, the vote was already being counted. Two old ladies were counting the forms onto the table.

"Ladies, how's it looking?" the general asked.

"Looks like it's going to be unanimous, sir. But we haven't had the votes from the three points yet," one of them said.

"Jenny, I don't think six against would make any difference, do you?" he said.

Jenny shook her head. "Then the vote stands in favour, sir," she said.

That was music to my ears, but Dad's earlier warning echoed in my mind - it was likely too late now.

Chapter Seven

The two mercenaries reached Kinkeel lough, a small lake, and were almost at the castle when the colonel's men caught them. They were taken totally by surprise and stripped of all their weapons and communication devices. The colonel's men took them to Bruce's cave, where they stripped them naked and gave them each a pair of swimming trunks to wear. The general wanted to question them personally and strictly forbade any communication, even though they pleaded innocence. They stewed in the cave, watching the rising tide draw closer to the solid steel bars that the general had installed to create a prison that would become totally immersed by the tide.

This was one of two caves called Bruce's cave. The second location, higher above sea level, avoids flooding from rising tides. During the building works for the first cave, they accidentally discovered the second one. To intimidate, the general would place someone in the first cave. For secure confinement, the second.

By morning, the invaders will succumb to either hypothermia or drowning.

"Who sent you?" came a voice into the cave.

Both mercenaries scanned their prison cell for the voice's source. An electronic device disguised the general's voice, making it sound different and slightly more threatening.

"Who sent you?" he asked again.

The two refused to speak.

"You may not have realized, but the tide is returning. This cave will fill in less than an hour, and you will both drown. The authorities will easily recognise, by your attire, that you both drowned due to foolishly swimming in the bay, which happens frequently in this area. I'll ask one more time. Who sent you?"

One of them had moved to the steel bars and tried his strength against them, to no avail. He hesitantly went back to his accomplice and glanced upward at the voice's origin.

"We're innocent hikers, just out for the day," he said.

"Well now, how many innocent hikers walk about with army issue handguns? A rookie mistake, Mr Banbury. That is your name, Roger Banbury. I know all about you and your army service. Quite an extensive history you've had over the years. Afghanistan, Croatia, and northern Ireland, and now you work as a gun for hire," the general stated.

"Who the fuck are you?" asked Banbury.

"And your colleague there, Mr Timpson. His experience differs from yours. He's one of those Xbox heroes who fancies his chances in the real world but has to rely on people like you to carry him the distance. He will be the first to drown. You can't swim, can you, Richard?"

Timpson looked furious. "Who the hell are you and what do you want from us?" he shouted.

"Stupid too. He's forgotten the question already. Oh, please catch-up, Xbox boy," the general said.

"If we tell you, will you let us go?" asked Banbury.

"No! However, we will ensure your transfer to a safe location until the authorities arrive."

"Then stuff you. We'll take our chances here," Banbury shouted.

"Then you will both drown with the evening's tide. Just another tragic accident," the general said.

Timpson moved closer to Banbury.

"For God's sake, let's tell them. I can't swim and you can't hold your breath long enough for the tide to go back out." He said.

"He's bluffing," Banbury stated.

"The tide has already reached the bars. Look," Timpson added.

He was right. The returning tide was lapping at the bars of the cave entrance.

"Now, the only way out is through that cell door. When the tide gets to the door, it's too late. My men will not get their feet wet. The choice is yours. You have ten minutes to decide," the general said sternly. "You mull it over while your feet get wet."

The general clicked the mic off, and it echoed around the cave. Banbury had to ensure there was no way out. He tried his strength against the door and the cave entrance bars. They were solid. Banbury wrapped his arms around himself to keep warm. The icy wind bringing in the tide was brutal, and they were no longer dressed for the climate.

The disguised voice was right. They were going to die if they didn't share some information. Remembering his training, he knew he had to do and say enough to survive capture and interrogation until rescued. Timpson was likely to spill the beans, so control the information flow.

"Ok, we'll tell you," Banbury shouted.

There was no reply. Only the sound of the tide against the bars and rocks.

"Hello, I want to tell you."

Still nothing. Stressed, Timpson moved closer to the voice's direction.

"Hello are you there? We wanna talk," Timpson yelled.

"Is it too late?" Timpson pleaded with Banbury.

"Ten minutes he said, now shut the fuck up whining. How did you ever get this job if you've had no fucking training?" Banbury asked.

"It was just a simple scouting mission, nothing else," said Timpson.

"Well, if you had any training you would have learned that not everything goes to plan and sometimes you need a Plan B," Banbury postured.

"Great, then what's your Plan B?"

"Not gonna happen unless we get out of here," Banbury said.

"Oh great. Now how far did your army training get you?" Timpson said sarcastically.

"Fuck off, Xbox boy, and let me think," Banbury shouted at him.

The returning tide was coming fast. It had already reached their feet, just a meter from the steel door. Cold water compelled both to find higher ground, escaping the sea's effects. Unless hyperthermia arrived first, Banbury believed they would drown. Either way, they had it.

The general hoped that when they could see for themselves that the tide filled the cave, they would reconsider. That is why he gave them the ten minutes. The click of the microphone was a welcome sound to them now.

"Have you decided?" the general asked them in his disguised voice.

"We'll tell you! Now get us out of here," Banbury shouted.

"Once you share the information, I'll get you out. Things aren't looking favourable to you, are they? Now stop wasting my time. Who sent you and who is paying you?" the general asked.

"Ok, it was Marco Dellucci. He's a drug kingpin from the Bristol area," Banbury said reluctantly.

"Tell me something new," the general stated.

"Why all the charades if you already know?" Timpson shouted.

"Who were you sent to kill?" the voice asked.

"Not kill, no. Just find and report back," Banbury said.

"Who?" the voice shouted.

"Just someone who witnessed a murder or something. Their faces are in my backpack if you check. Bruce someone, and his girlfriend," Banbury said.

There was a long pause.

"Hello?" Timpson shouted. "You got what you wanted. Now get us out of here."

"I believe you are telling the truth. How were you expected to report back if you didn't find them here?" the voice asked.

"By phone, in my bag, too. But they don't know we are here. I couldn't get any signal when we got off the ferry," Banbury added.

"I keep it that way. We can communicate with the outside world through other methods. It appears you are no longer a threat to us, and no further use to us. Goodbye."

Those words sent a panic through their minds. Suddenly, they believed they were lied to and left to die. Both of them screamed at the voice, pleading for their lives.

In the control room, the general had a smile. "I love this bit when they panic," he said.

"You're not going to leave them there, are you?" I asked him.

"This is war Bruce. In war there are casualties. If we let them go, they will tell everyone, and soon we will be inundated with mercenaries. It is best to leave them where they are and let a tragic accident happen to them, so that their families can still receive compensation."

"Yes, right, of course you are. Now, what are you really going to do with them?" I asked him.

"I have no plans for them, other than they stay where they are."

"You can't just murder them," I pleaded.

The general looked at me and took my shoulders in his hands.

"Son, how did you think this was going to turn out? Ultimately, it's going to come down to them, or us. Them, or you and Janie. If they stay where they are, we have two fewer enemies to worry about," Dad said with authority.

"Then we are no better than they are. This isn't the Falkland's dad; this is civilian life. Keep them prisoners until it ends, then hand them over to the proper authorities for trial."

"In the meantime, I have to feed them and clothe them and see to their medical needs. Taking men off the front line of defending this place to make sure they don't escape and attack us from inside the compound." He was getting annoyed with me.

"Yes, if that's what it takes," I stated. "This is not a conflict sanctioned by the home office. You will have to answer for your actions in the real world. Let's make them honourable."

"Son, I am so pleased your mother brought you up right with good moral principles…"

"…don't mention her. You have no right to even say her name," I retorted.

"You don't get it; this is a matter of life or death. You and Janie came here because you wanted me to keep you safe and protect you. So let me do the job you asked of me," he said. "Every single person here voted to help you, knowing that they may have to pay for the ultimate sacrifice in doing so. They know what it means to be in a conflict with others who think that the rules don't matter to them. People like this, Marco, think that they are invincible, and their money can buy them anything or anybody they want. We have come across people like this all over the world. Your government, who makes the rules you want us to adhere to, usually instructs us to take them out. Kill them without prejudice. That's the order we get to carry out from your law makers. They are no more honourable than Marco, and his kind are."

His words were hitting home. He was right, and I so didn't want him to be. He could see I was digesting his lecture.

"Look, son, think of how many people will be glad that this asshole can no longer inflict all the pain and misery he does. All the little kids these drug dealers ruin the lives of with their filthy product. Think about the families of these kids ruined by it. The lives of the addicts they create to sell their product to. The world is always a better place without people like them. So, with respect, son, leave your morals at the drawbridge or cross it," he said.

"So, there is no other way?" I asked, in a last ditched attempt to reason with him.

"Look, alright, I'll put those two under lock and key for the time being. But, if this Marco asshole comes calling, then I promise you, anyone who takes arms against us will meet with deadly resistance," he said with a smile. "Freddy, put them in cave number two and give them a blanket," he added.

I know what he was trying to do. He was trying to save face in front of his men. He was right, and I know he was right about everything he said. I just can't stand to see anyone hurt. I'm the type of guy who would cross the road to help a complete stranger if they needed it. If I was any different, then maybe I would have followed in his footsteps and signed up, instead of going to university to get my master's degree in mathematics.

The general had asked for their backpack to retrieve the phone they said they had in it. He wanted to check that they were telling the truth about not reporting back. Colonel Rogers brought it to him. Before departing the mainland, they mentioned their plans to visit the island. A text was sent to an anonymous number. They assumed it was Marco or one of his lieutenants, as they're called.

"Damn it," the general said.

"What's the matter?" I asked him.

"They told Marco that they were coming to the island. So now, if they return, they will tell them all about us. If they don't return, they will assume you are here or will send others to find out what happened," he instructed.

He placed the phone on the table next to Freddy.

"Try to find out what you can from the phone. You know, anything useful," he asked.

"Yes sir," said Freddy.

"Colonel Rogers, you get word to the three points and make sure they have everything they need. Food, guns, ammunition, night vision, everything."

"Yes sir," said the colonel, and took the stairs up.

"What are the three points?" I asked the general.

"Freddy, call up a map of the island," he instructed.

By pressing buttons on his consul, Freddy displayed a map of the island on the main screen. It was an odd shape, like a boomerang. The general touched the extremities of the island. It was obvious what the three points were when I saw the map. The three points were the bottom right and left and the middle top parts of the island.

"The three points are all lighthouses that keep shipping safe. We took over control of them when we bought the island as a means of an advanced warning system. They were a bit run down, so we fixed them up and offered to man them and maintain them. The islanders had no objections and were grateful we did. Our men have been watching the horizons ever since. When they come, we will have about thirty minutes' warning."

"What if they come by air, not water," I stupidly asked.

"Really?" the general asked sarcastically. "The same. Except they will get here faster," he added.

It was a stupid question, but he forgot I'm not a military man. I thought I was being helpful.

"They won't be coming by air. Helicopters are too expensive to run, and you have to log flight plans, etc. His kind don't want anyone knowing where they are or how they travel," said Freddy.

"That's right. Our chopper was over six million and costs us over a hundred thousand a year to run and maintain it," the general said nonchalantly.

"Oh yes, you said you have a chopper?" I stated.

"Yes, we have one of those Apaches. We only got the mark one and not one of those new-fangled version six. What is it Freddy? The Ah-64E's?" the general asked.

Freddy nodded.

"Oh, only the mark one," I said sarcastically.

"Yes, that's right, sir. Oh, and do you want to move it to the east point lighthouse as we rehearsed?" asked Freddy.

"Yes, good idea. Get the Wombat to take her out and wait with the east point team," he agreed.

"The Wombat?" I asked.

"You met her this morning. Jenny, who did the votes. She has been flying choppers since you were in nappies. Hell of a pilot. As brave as they come. Got us out of a few nasty scrapes, I can tell you," he said.

The more I heard of this rag-tag army of his, the more they impressed me. They were so organised. It would be unwise for Marco to attempt anything here. These guys can wipe him from the planet. But Marco doesn't know what he will be up against. So, if he discovers his men missing, he will come without knowing that the deck is stacked against him.

"Sound general alert Freddy. Assemble everyone in full gear on the parade ground in thirty minutes or after the helicopter departs. We need to prepare for the inevitable," the general ordered.

He looked at me. "You need to get back with Janie and let her know what's going on. She may get scared when the alarm sounds," he said.

"I want to be of help. What can I do?" I asked.

"You have your orders, son; I'll call you if I need you to do something. Look after Janie," he barked.

"Yes, sir," I replied disappointedly.

I turned to mount the stairs.

"Oh, and son?" he called after me.

I turned to face him.

"It's good to have you here. When this is over, I'd like us to get to know each other again," he smiled.

"I'd like that too, dad," I said and climbed the stairs.

The sonic alarm wasn't excessively loud, but its volume carried uniformly across the castle. It was the same amount of noise upstairs as it was down. People rushed around me, disappearing into rooms along every corridor I walked. Janie was there, waiting at the door, when I arrived. I ushered her in to explain.

"Dad has sounded general alert, and they are preparing to fight with Marco and his guys. He wants to be prepared when they arrive. If they get here."

"What do you mean, if they get here?" she asked me.

"Well, we don't really know for sure that they are coming. We just think he will come when he finds out two of his men are missing," I said.

"Are two of his men missing?" she asked.

"Yes, dad has them naked in the dungeon."

"Why naked? Is he a pervert or something like his son? They'll freeze to death in this weather," she said with a smile.

"I am not a pervert," I smiled back. "Anyway, that was the point; to extract information from them. They came on this morning's ferry, sent by Marco, looking for us."

"Well, let them freeze. Bastards," she snarled.

"You know, even though I'm scared to death of what's going to happen, it's fucking exhilarating," I said excitedly. "Dads got a fucking Apache helicopter and everything," I was getting a little lightheaded. Jannie could tell.

"Come on, sit down before you hyperventilate. Calm yourself and stop fucking swearing," she said, sitting on the bed and patting the space next to her.

I sat beside her and tried to relax, but the sonic alarm was a constant reminder of what was going to happen. I struggled to calm down, fearing the need for a paper bag. It had happened once before in the office. I can't remember what set me off, but I remember the reason I gained control again. She was brilliant under pressure. Well, then, anyway. Now, the stakes are a lot higher, too high, if you were asking me.

Janie waited, taking every breath with me; trying to slow my breathing down until I had completely calmed down, before she began speaking again.

"Better?" she asked.

I was better and felt like we had avoided another crisis.

"What is our task during this general alert? Did he tell you?" she asked.

"He told me to come to you, in case you were getting scared, and to wait here until he asked for me. That's if he needs me," I said.

"So, what do we do while we wait, then?" she asked. "Maybe we should have a fuck. This might be our last chance," she added.

"You're a horny bitch!" I said, hardly getting the words out of my mouth before she lunged at me, forcing me to lie on the bed. She kissed me. That was all I needed to get me going.

Chapter Eight

We lay in the bed, out of breath, and Janie had her head on my chest. I was admiring the flames of the fire dancing in the fireplace.

"When did they come and light the fire?" I asked her.

"My friend from dinner, Henry; he came and set it while you were with your dad this morning. He's a funny bugger. Had me in stitches chatting about your dad and the chicken in Kabul," she replied.

"Dad and the chicken in Kabul? I haven't heard that one yet."

"You must get your dad to tell you, it's hilarious," she added.

The sound of the Apache helicopter taking off made us scramble to the window, hoping to catch a glimpse. Suddenly, the cold air hit our naked bodies, and we ran back to the bed, throwing ourselves under the bedding.

"We better get dressed and head downstairs. It'll be dinnertime soon," I said.

"If everyone is on alert, will there be any?" she asked.

"Well, I assume so. They've got to eat. An army doesn't fight on an empty stomach and all that," I said.

There had to be something. Even if only bread and sandwich ingredients. We quickly dressed and left our room. There was no noise at all. No people running about, no sonic alarm. We passed through the usual hallways and nothing. The dining room was empty, too. Where were they all? Then we heard the stamping of feet on gravel, many feet. The soldiers were on parade in the centre bailey. I think that's what they call it. The castle's central area, enclosed by walls. That's where they must have kept the helicopter. When we arrived, we entered the castle by the barbican and then went straight inside to the accommodations areas.

The walls of this castle, unlike most other ones I have seen, house the accommodations, making them about twenty feet wide. They were also two stories high, making the walls thirty feet high, with turrets on top again. Exterior walls, I was told, are eight feet thick at the base. Also, they made all exterior walls from granite, making this place solid and hard to breach. Modern day explosives would chew a hole in them pretty fast, but you would have to get close enough to lay the charges. In the olden days, that is when they would pour oil onto the intruders and set them alight or throw rocks and boulders at them from the turrets. I'm not sure if Dad has any plans like that, but it wouldn't surprise me.

Only the kitchen bustled with activity, as three people worked hard to prepare sandwiches and stuff them into foil bags. Three people were hard at work preparing sandwiches and stuffing them into foil bags.

"What's going on? No cooked meal today for them?" I asked.

"No, they should be on army ration packs, but everyone voted against them. Instead, we are making the ration packs ourselves. We could do with some help if you're not doing anything," the chef said.

"Sure, of course we will," Janie said, making her way around to the other side of the large stainless-steel table. "I'm Janie and this is Bruce," she continued.

"I'm Jackie, and he's Thomas, and we have another Jackie over there. So just call me chef, less confusing," said the chef.

"Right, chef. What do you need us to do?" asked Janie.

"If you can slice up that bag of tomatoes, please, and Bruce, if you want to help Jackie put them into the bags, we'll have it all covered. Thanks," instructed chef.

"First, wash your hands," called out Jackie, from the back.

We washed our hands and dried them with the blue paper towel from the roll dispenser on the wall. We started our tasks, and it was nice to be helping, instead of just watching everyone else do it all.

"How many of these do you have to make?" I asked.

"Two hundred," the chef said.

"Yes, right, but how many really?" I quipped.

"Two hundred. We will put one hundred in the fridge and distribute the other hundred as soon as everyone completes their tasks for today."

"How many mouths to feed are there?" Janie asked.

"Fifty-seven; but seven of those are self-contained in the three points. So, one hundred is just two packs each, which is dinner and tea tonight," she said. "Fifty ham and tomato, fifty cheese and mustard, fifty corned beef, and we haven't decided on the last lot yet. Not sure what we got," she added.

"We'll be here all day," I said.

"Ow, tosh. Two hours tops," said Thomas.

While getting started on the task, I was curious to know more about these individuals.

"In the army, Jackie, what did you do?" I asked the lady next to me.

"Catering corps, well, it's called Royal Logistics now," she replied.

"And is this what you do here?" I asked.

"We work in shifts, three days on and three days off, the chef and me. It's a full-time job feeding this lot, but no different from when we were serving, I suppose," she said.

"Back then, we used to feed several hundred hungry soldiers in every part of the globe," chef added.

"What about you, Thomas? What did you do?" asked Janie of him.

"Communications then, and I share the den with Freddy now," he said.

"Oh yes! You were in the den with Freddy when I first went down there."

"Any way guys, let's get cracking. I'm due back in the den in an hour," said Thomas.

"I've got to ask someone, and I hope you guys don't mind, but basically you are all rich from the treasure hunt. Why not explore a warmer climate instead of staying here?"

"One word, family," said the chef.

"Family?" I asked.

"These guys are our family. We have done so much together and have shared so many good times and bad times together. We are like one big, happy family," said the chef.

"That's fair enough. I can understand that," I said.

We cut, buttered, stacked, and bagged furiously for the next hour until Thomas had to leave. We were almost done; the fridge was fully stocked, and we had just about finished them all, when a voice came over the speakers that were used to emit the sonic alarm.

"Bruce Rankin, please come to the den. Bruce Rankin to the den." It was Freddy's voice.

I looked at the chef and Janie, sorry for having to leave them.

"You go, we got this," said Janie.

"Sorry girls," I said.

"Here, take one with you. You haven't eaten yet," said the chef, holding out a bagged sandwich.

"Thank you," I said, kissed Janie and left for the den.

When I got to the den, there wasn't much room in there. The general and both colonels were standing, hovering, behind Freddy and Thomas sat at the controls. As I entered, Dad heard me and looked in my direction before returning his attention to the screens.

"Bruce, recognize any of these men?" the general asked. "Call them up Freddy."

Four men appeared on the screen. Three I didn't know.

"I know that face," I said. "Top left. He was the man with Marco when he shot my boss, but I don't recognise the other ones," I said.

"I believe they're a recon team searching for the missing duo," the general said.

My heart sank a little. I knew they would come but hoped that they wouldn't.

"Where are they?" I asked him.

"They just got off the ferry and are heading towards us," he said.

"Sir, they are tracking them," Thomas pipped in.

"I agree sir, they are tracking them by their phones or something," added Freddy.

"I thought that all phone signals had been turned off," the general said.

"They are, but that one is holding a directional finder and is definitely tracking somehow," stated Freddy, pointing at the guy I recognised.

"We know who they are and why they're here, but what now?" said dad. "Options?" he added.

"Take them out of the game and put them with the other two," said Colonel Rogers.

"Fisher, you seem quiet. What do you think?" asked the general of the other colonel.

"Six trained men in our cells together, is just asking for trouble. We should discover their tracking target and swiftly transport it to the other side of the island on Rosemary."

"Yes, I like that. Are we agreed?" asked the general.

Both colonels nodded.

"Right then, Freddy, can you scan for whatever signal they are tracking and locate it?"

"Already on it, sir," he said.

Freddy and Thomas expertly scanned the island, trying to zero in on the target.

"Found it, sir. It's not a mobile device, it's a homing beacon. The two mercs must have activated it when they were first caught," said Thomas.

"Good man, can you pinpoint it? We need to take it out of play," the general asked.

"It's by the small lake, Kinkeel, Sir," Freddy said.

"Right where we picked them up, sir. Sorry we missed it. I take full responsibility for it," said Colonel Fisher. "I'll take it out, sir, personally," he added.

"Thank you, colonel," said the general.

"Sir, if we get Rosemary in Arkill bay, we may still lead them away. I can use a drone to send it to her, and she can take it across the island," Fisher added.

"Good idea Fisher. Make it happen," the general instructed.

"Who's Rosemary?" I had to ask.

"She is our Defiant-class patrol vessel. We use her to fetch supplies from the mainland with no questions asked," he replied. "Our naval contingent, if you like," he added.

"Of course, you have a boat as well," I said sarcastically.

"We live on an island, Bruce. Why wouldn't we have a boat?" he replied, with as much sarcasm.

Another stupid question, of course they would. Either the islanders own a boat, or they become isolated on the island. As the drawbridge was dropped, we watched the monitors and saw the colonel and two others leaping out on dirt bikes. We waited for the signal to move, indicating that the colonel had retrieved it and was heading for the bay. It felt like forever before Fisher responded.

"Fisher to control, over."

The general grabbed the radio mouthpiece. "Go ahead, Fisher, over," he replied.

"Fisher to control, target is compromised. Repeat target is compromised. Permission to engage? Over."

"Negative Fisher, do not engage unless fired upon, over."

"Understood, control. What are my orders, sir? Over."

"Stand by Fisher, over," the general said and threw the mouthpiece down on the desk.

Freddy replaced the mouthpiece into its holder.

"If we take them out, everyone will come. If we don't, these four will eventually discover their friends in Bruce's cave, and everyone will still come. Options?" the general demanded.

"Sir, they are mercs. Could we buy them off?" the colonel asked.

"We could, but if they disappear, we still got the rest coming. I need an option where everything ends here, so we don't have to go into battle," said the general.

"What if we call the police and say armed men are on the island in force? They would have to deal with it. Then all we have to worry about is the time it takes the police armed response to get here," I told him.

"I like that better, but didn't you say they had the police in their pockets?" the general replied, looking at me.

"Well, I think so. But that was in Bristol. This is a long way from Bristol," I stated.

The general thought for a moment. "Colonel, what do you think?"

"My only worry would be if the police are bent, they could twist the call out and we could also face the armed police. They are civilians doing a job, sir. I would rather not involve them. Especially if they end up on the other side," said the colonel.

"Very wise. He makes a point Bruce," the general said.

"Though I hate to admit it, I think I agree with the colonel when you put it that way," I said.

"Then it's agreed. We go to war," the general said and retrieved the radio mouthpiece. "Control to Fisher."

"Fisher receiving, go ahead control, over."

"Take them out Fisher. I repeat, eliminate the targets, and hide the bodies. No trace. Do you copy, over?"

"Well, hang on Dad, that's drastic isn't it? Throw them in the dungeon, too. You don't have to kill them."

"They are coming anyway, Bruce. There will be no stopping them now. This Marco character must choose between eliminating you and Janie or enduring a life of captivity. He will stop at nothing short of killing you both. Do you understand that?"

"Yes, but is killing them actually necessary?" I pleaded.

"The rules of combat are very simple, Bruce. Kill or be killed. I didn't live this long by patting the enemy on the back and getting them to promise not to do it again," he said, raising his voice. "I suggest you make yourself useful in the kitchen and leave the waring to us."

Of course, he was right. I knew he was right. But I have been brought up better than that. I moved towards the stairs and started climbing as the radio buzzed to life once more.

"Fisher to control, targets eliminated. I repeat, targets eliminated."

"Control to Fisher, message received. Wrap up and return to control, over."

"All received. Over and out."

I had to stop this madness somehow. By the time I got to the top of the stairs, I was fuming. All these people getting killed because of me and Janie. No, because of me. I was the one who saw everything. I wish I hadn't, but it's too late for that now. I was not happy with the situation, but less happy with all the wanton murder. I just couldn't see past the fact that these intruders had families, wives, kids, parents. They're the ones that will suffer the most.

Dad would probably argue that when you join the army, that was a possibility you signed up for. But these guys were not in the army. I supposed they should have known something could happen to them being part of Marco's drug empire. I supposed they should have known by the cut of their employer that they were already on the wrong side of the law. But nobody expects that to happen. All they see is the rewards of success; and in the drugs empire, the rewards are high.

Janie saw me marching past the kitchen door and ran after me.

"Bruce, what's wrong?" she asked, grabbing my arm to stop me from racing.

"This whole thing has gone too far. He just executed four of Marco's men. God knows what he'll do to them in the cave, assuming they're still alive."

"Bruce, what did you think was going to happen?" she asked.

"What? I don't know. Not murder for no reason."

"You need to calm down, Bruce." She grabbed a chair from the dining table and pulled it to her. "Sit!" she demanded.

Her order shocked me, and I sat down, not taking my eyes from hers.

"Of course, people are going to die. Be killed, executed, shot, burned, and blown up. These men of Marco's have come here for one reason. To kill us. Now grow some fucking balls, babe."

She crouched down beside me.

"This is a situation where it's kill or be killed," she added.

"You're beginning to sound like my father," I interjected.

"I agree with him. I'm relieved the enemy is dying instead of these wonderful people. Marco usually meets no resistance and kills when and where ever he feels like it. He thinks he is above the law and can avoid justice by killing everything in his way. The difference now is that he faces a force willing to confront and beat him at his own game."

Of course, she was making sense, but I still felt all they were doing was justifying murder.

"It just goes against everything I have ever known and believed. It's hard to get my head around," I said.

She took my hands in hers.

"Look, if we were still in Bristol, we would be dead by now. Marco would have had us shot and gotten away with it. He would escape punishment for killing Hamilton, Doug, and Celine. Five murders with no justice at all, and God knows how many more he has, or will commit in the future, just to keep causing misery to all the people addicted to his drugs, just to line his pockets with gold. He must pay for everything, but with the police under his control, it's unlikely he ever will by any other method. So, don't you dare feel sorry for them. I don't."

Ah fuck! She is right, too. Then it's me. I'm the stupid one. Her words cut me like a knife. I need to grow some balls, as she put it. We cuddled, and the tension melted away. They were all right, and they were the professionals. I would have been pissed off if they had tried to tell me how to keep accurate accounts. Oh, that does sound lame. I smiled at her, and we kissed.

"You are right, I am wrong. Sorry," I said to her.

"We are all wrong, but this way is the lesser of two evils," she said.

"I can see that now, thank you, and I'm sorry," I said.

"Don't apologise," she said, standing. "Just get your sexy little ass in that kitchen and finish your work," she said, slapping my ass.

Suddenly, a thought leaped into my head. Not sure where from. I stopped in my tracks and looked blankly at Janie. I think she thought I was having a heart attack or something.

"My God, Bruce, what's wrong? Are you alright?" she asked.

"The islanders," I said, and raced back to the control room. I flew down the stairs and at the bottom, I had to catch my breath.

"Dad, the islanders," I said between breaths.

"What about them?" he asked.

"The other islanders could get hurt if Marco's force goes towards the homing beacon first. I think we should bring their signal here to the castle to make sure that Marco heads in the right direction and minimizes the civilian casualties. Unless you are going to evacuate them all?"

"Now you're thinking like a soldier, son. He grabbed the radio mic."

"Control to Fisher, control to Fisher."

"Fisher receiving, go ahead control, over." Came the reply.

"Fisher, grab that homing beacon of theirs and bring it back to the castle intact. I repeat, bring their homing beacon back to base intact, over!" the general ordered.

"Fisher to control, received, out."

"Bloody good idea, son, thank you," Dad said.

Well, now I felt better, as I probably saved a few lives. Good for me.

Chapter Nine

We spent the rest of the evening distributing the home-made ration packs to all the residents. Residents, that seems to be a word that no longer fits, given the day's events. We'll call them troops from now on. I couldn't help but say thank you to everyone I passed a foil bag to. I was grateful that they were willing to put their lives on the line for me and Janie. Radios were distributed where directed, facilitating better communication for all. We spread the news of a meeting in the dining room at 1800 hours for all troops.

The meeting came around fast. All stood in formation in the dining room and stood to attention when the general entered with his two colonels.

"Stand easy, men!" Fisher said. Then looked to the general as if it was his turn to speak.

"Thank you colonel. There has been a development, and we are now officially at war. A small scouting party has been eliminated this morning, and it is agreed that we may expect a larger force to follow. We must not underestimate this force when it comes. They may be civilian based, but they are expected to have their ranks swollen with mercs. I want everyone to prepare the island for an invading force. Just like we practiced," he stated.

A soldier in the front raised his hand.

"Go ahead sergeant," the general said.

"Sir, do we know numbers?" he asked.

The general looked at me. I used my body language to say I have no idea.

"We may not know until one of the three points gives us our thirty-minute warning. Everyone, it's time to prepare. Phase one, gardeners; let's get the land prepared to repel invaders. Cover and prepare all points of entry. Ornithologists, prepare your hides with all the ammo and everything you need for phase two. Knitters, prepare for close quarters combat and if you can help the gardeners, please do so. Everyone else, prepare the castle for invaders. Stock the turrets and warm the pots," the general said.

He turned and looked at each of the colonels. They stood to attention before him. The general stepped forward towards his aging troops. Obedient and ready for action, they stood before him. Their smart uniforms were ill-fitting and outdated; their helmets and berets looked balanced on grey and silver-haired, frail looking heads. They looked more like a remembrance day parade than a fighting force.

"Now ladies and gents, friends, and family; we may not be as young or as fresh faced as we were back when we served."

The general walked between his troops, putting his hands on their shoulders and tweaking their appearances as he spoke.

"We may not be as sharp as we were. But we have age and experience and a wealth of knowledge on our side. We have accomplished more, defeated more enemies, and forgotten more than these drug users will ever know. We have trained specifically for this day, and we are more prepared, more equipped, and more resilient than those who come for us. We have fought in some inhumane conditions and situations that would make these snowflakes puke and run back to their mummies. We are the ultimate fighting machine, but we are not fighting just to protect the innocents this time; we are fighting for justice, and our home."

The general looked sombre and walked back to the front of his troops and stood between his two colonels.

"Now, we may lose some friends today, our family, but they will have died for a higher cause and will be remembered for serving our kind of justice and for showing these bastards that they cannot get away with it any longer. It's time for them to pay the piper."

An enormous cheer enveloped the room. Hands thrown into the air with clenched fists.

"The general raised his hands for silence and the room fell quiet.

"Let's prepare for war," he added.

Colonel Rogers stepped forward. "Sergeant Walker?"

The sergeant understood what should happen next without the last command. He stepped forward and saluted his three superiors, who returned the gesture. He turned to face the troops.

"Attention!" he shouted.

All the troops stamped their left feet and stood to attention as best they could, some with canes and walking sticks in hand.

"You have your orders. Now make it happen. To the right, dismissed."

All the troops turned to their right and stamped their feet in unison, then dissolved into a mass of moving bodies towards the door.

An organised chaos ensued; people were everywhere inside and outside the castle. Outside, the gardening club was busy digging holes and laying mines. They stood hundreds of garden gnomes on the plush green grass verge between the castle walls and the curtain walls all around the castle. What purpose they served, I wasn't sure, but they made the castle look more homely.

All four corners of the castle held sniper nests atop their towers. They strategically positioned boxes of ammunition and grenades all around the battlements. Quad bikes, with trailers filled with boxes, crossed the drawbridge, for destinations unknown to me. At a guess, I would have said they were for the ornithologist's hides dotted around the island.

I saw two old soldiers crossing the drawbridge carrying two large, round tin containers each, labelled cooking oil.

One headed towards the cliff at Doon bay and the other towards Arkill bay. Large rocks and boulders from the bay were brought back by the returning quad bikes and hoisted to the battlements on pulley systems. They were heavy enough to pick up, but I couldn't see any of these aged soldiers throwing them. So, again, I was not sure of their usage.

Several hours later, everything was still and quiet. Everyone was at their posts, prepared and ready for action. The radios fell silent. I joined the general and his two colonels in the control room, and we all sat and watched the screen for any signs of movement. Three hours passed, and I was bored out of my head. Never had I been required to remain so still and silent for such a prolonged period. It felt like I was back at school during an exam.

The phone rang, and I jumped in response to it. Freddy answered it.

"Castle retirement home. How can I help you?" Freddy said.

"Yes, ok, are you sure? Ok. All received, thank you Chloe," he added.

"Sir, Chloe from the harbourside café in Bally Castle said an armed force of about twenty men have commandeered boats and have entered the water. She said she can't tell where they are going, but thought we should know," Freddy continued.

"So, this is going to happen, after all?" I asked.

The general stood. "Okay, Freddy, get Rosemary and the Wombat to intercept. Do not engage unless fired upon. Give them the option to turn around and go home," he instructed.

Freddy grabbed the radio mic and spoke.

"Control to Wombat, control to Wombat, are you receiving? Over?"

After a moment of silence, a voice spoke up.

"Wombat to control, receiving loud and clear, over."

"Control to Wombat, intercept armed force entering the Rathlin Sound. Do not engage unless fired upon. Give them fair warning, over," said Freddy.

"Understood, Wombat out."

"Control to Rosemary, do you copy?" continued Freddy.

"Go ahead for Rosemary," came the reply.

"Rosemary, intercept invading force in the Rathlin sound, do not engage unless fired upon. Also, be aware Wombat is on route. I repeat, Wombat is on route, over."

"Control, this is Rosemary headed for the sound, will watch for Wombat, over and out." Came the brief reply.

"So, it has started? Hopefully, when they see Rosemary and that helicopter of yours, they will shit themselves and turn tail," I joked.

"I doubt it, son. We have fought a drug empire before in Afghanistan. Their men can be more dangerous than mercenaries, as they fear their leaders more than us. And that is a stupid combination, especially when you suddenly give them a weapon they're not trained with and throw them out of their comfort zone. Usually, there is only one outcome. A bloody one," The general stated.

"At the moment, they don't know the full extent of what they are up against," said Colonel Rogers. "But they soon will," he added.

"Switch to mission cameras," the general ordered.

Screens showed Wombat's pilot's view and Rosemary's cabin crew's ocean view.

A voice on the radio said, "Rue Point to control, over."

Freddy replied. "Go ahead Rue Point, receiving over."

"Rue point, to control, we have three vessels headed towards east of the island. I repeat headed for east of island towards Arkill and Doon bays over."

"Received Rue Point, over and out," replied Freddy.

The general looked at his colonels. He removed some banknotes from his pocket, held together with a gold clip. He removed two twenty-pound notes and gave them one each.

"Damn it, you guys are good," he said.

The colonels looked at each other and smiled, stuffing the money in their pockets. The general grabbed the mic from Freddy.

"Rosemary and Wombat, three vessels are heading to Arkill and Doon. Repeat Arkill and Doon, over."

"Rosemary received, over."

"Wombat received, over."

"Try to intercept before they crash on the rocks," the general added.

"Wombat two minutes out."

"Rosemary, two minutes out," came the replies.

* * *

Three small leisure crafts were bobbing up and down uncontrollably with the waves; five men in each craft huddled together cold and wet from the late crossing. Crossing against the tide is hazardous, so locals rarely left their moorings during those times. However, locals did not pilot these crafts. These were invaders hell bent on killing two people on the orders of their leader, Marco Dellucci.

His empire controlled the flow of all the cocaine and cannabis throughout the whole of the U.K. Estimates suggested that his empire was worth seven billion pounds a year and that three thousand individuals worked for or with him. Every time the police got close to him, he would receive a tip-off and successfully evade capture. Every time he was close to being arrested and tried for murder or drugs charges, the witnesses would disappear without a trace and turn up months later, dead.

Obviously, they had planned the same for Bruce and Janie. They had seen Marco himself shoot and kill a man in cold blood. So, now he was leaving nothing to chance. The last two attempts to silence them had failed, but this time was different. He was sending fifteen of his best men to finish the job once and for all.

Chapter Ten

Fifteen men in three small vessels heading for the beach at Doon bay. Locals know that the unseen rocks beneath the waves will not allow any craft except modern hovercrafts to land there. Boats get torn apart on the rocks, especially when trying to land against the tide. Their inexperience of these waters was going to kill them before they reached the island.

The lead vessel was a forty-one-foot Princess 412, meant for angling in calmer waters around Bally Castle at the western side of the island. Not meant for the rougher waters of the North Atlantic. It had the deepest draft of around a metre and would be the first to run aground on the rocks if they continued their journey towards Doon Bay.

Aboard the Princess, the men fell silent to the sounds of the approaching rotors of the Apache and the deep throbbing motor of the Defiant-class patrol vessel. They didn't know if they should look up or out to the sea behind them. Both crafts stopped in front of the Princess, keeping the invaders from moving onward.

"This is a restricted zone. Turnabout," bellowed the voice from the Apache attack helicopter.

The two smaller vessels caught up with the princess. And pulled alongside it.

"This is a restricted zone. Turnabout. This is your only warning."

Common sense would have led them to flee back to the mainland. But these were not your average individuals. These were men hired to do a job and feared the man paying the wages more than the defending force. Only the Apache's rotors broke the silence.

The Defiant's .50 calibre heavy machine gun was ready to use. What the invaders didn't know was it was as old as the soldiers manning it. Over the years, it had been well maintained and was well stocked. The invaders knew they were the target as they heard the weapon being prepared to fire. The heavy clunking of the loading system was enough warning.

Two smaller crafts revved their engines and turned about, heading back towards the mainland. The Princess did not move. The crew of the Rosemary fired a warning burst across its bow, despite that, it didn't move. Two small crafts moved farther away, becoming tiny dots on the horizon.

"Do you need a tow back to port?" bellowed the Wombat from inside the Apache.

Suddenly, the five men inside the Princess grabbed their assault rifles and machine guns and aimed them at the Apache. They fired into the air. The Apache aircraft withdrew and ascended, unleashing its firepower upon the princess, accompanied by Rosemary. Within seconds, their guns were silenced, and all five invaders were dead. The Princess sank into the waves and rested on the rocks below them. Half in and half out of the sea, balanced and wrecked on the rocks. Now a memorial and reminder to unwelcomed visitors.

Rosemary fired its engines and headed to the last seen position of the other two vessels. It was going to escort them back to port just in case they changed their minds. The Wombat flew the Apache over the Princess using its infrared camera to check for heat signatures or life. Having seen none, it flew over Rosemary and was going to do one flyby of the two smaller boats before heading back to base at the east point.

Back in the den, the Wombat had relayed the news to the General. He felt let down by the events, but I wasn't sure if it was because they destroyed one vessel or because it was just one of them.

"Thank you, Wombat. Return to base, over," the general said into the radio. "Control to Rosemary, over," he continued.

"Go for Rosemary," came the reply.

"Rosemary, when the port of Bally is in site, stand ready in the Sound and monitor the situation from there, over," he said.

"Rosemary to control, message received five by five, will monitor until further instructions, out," came the reply.

The general replaced the microphone on the radio hook and looked puzzled.

"Dad, what's the matter?" I asked him.

He looked at me and said nothing.

"Freddy, have we been monitoring the police frequencies?" the general asked.

"Yes, sir," said Freddy.

"Has there been nothing on it at all? Surely someone reported the theft of the boats from Bally. Someone must have heard the Wombat, or Rosemary at least."

"No sir, nothing at all. Everything is quiet," Freddy replied.

"Is that a bad thing?" I asked.

"Let's say it's unusual. The other islanders are unfamiliar with our intentions. When we engage in war games and practice our craft, we typically attract the attention of the boys in blue," said the general.

"Isn't it a bit early for that yet?" I quizzed.

"You may be right. Let's wait and see what happens in the next couple of hours," he said. "Freddy, give Rosemary an hour, then bring her back to base."

"Yes, Sir," Freddy replied.

"Oh, Freddy, when Rosemary is back at base, stand the troops down to tactical two!" the general commanded.

"Tactical two, aye, Sir."

"What is tactical two?" I asked, to anybody who would answer.

"The troops stand down from the ready. They still man their posts, but only one per post and relieve each other so that everyone gets a hot meal and a break," said Colonel Fisher.

"But isn't it all over now?" I asked.

"Who knows for sure? My guess is not. But only time will tell," said the general.

"I agree sir, they'll go back with their tails between their legs, regroup and try again," said Colonel Fisher.

I had to agree with them; that seemed a little too easy.

"They're trying us out to see what they are up against," said Colonel Rogers, who had been silent up to now.

"Yes, that would be the logical approach. But are they organised enough?" asked the general.

"If they have a large number of mercenaries in their ranks, they could be, sir," Fisher added.

The general talked to his colonels. "You two run a critical eye over everything. Double check all our defences and get group leaders to run through what they have done. See if we have any weak spots we need to bolster."

They saluted and disappeared up the stairs.

"Can I help dad?" I asked him.

"I need you to stay out of sight in case they have a sniper we miss. I think it best if you and Janie take cell number one down here to be safe," he said. "Bring her down with drinks and supplies as needed. You may be here for some time."

He immediately looked away and touched Freddy on his shoulder. Thomas sat in the chair next to him and looked up at his commanding officer.

"Lock the island down. Lock the castle down. Inform all troops that the east side tunnel will remain open and to use discretion while utilising it. Tell the three points that we are going to red alert and report back on anything that looks suspicious," the general commanded.

Dad turned back to me and seemed annoyed that I was still there.

"Move quickly, son. We don't know how long until it starts again."

I nodded in agreement and mounted the stairs. I rushed up three flights to my room, hoping Janie would be there. She wasn't in the kitchen when I passed. I arrived at our bedroom door and tried to open it, but it was locked.

Thankfully, that meant that Janie was inside. I knocked and called out.

"Janie it's me, Bruce."

There was no answer. She had to be there. If not, how did the door get locked? I bashed at the door louder and harder.

"Janie! Open up, it's Bruce," I called.

I could hear rustling from behind the door. The lock rang out, and the door opened. There stood a tired-looking Janie rubbing her eyes.

"Sorry, I must have fallen asleep," she said.

"How can you sleep at a time like this?" I asked her.

"I was bored, alright!" she snapped a little impatiently.

I entered the room and closed the door behind me.

"The general, sorry my dad, wants us to keep out of sight and sleep and stay in the den in case they have snipers or something," I relayed.

"Why? What has happened?" she quizzed.

"Oh, yes, of course. You don't know. Their Apache helicopter and assault boat thing opened fire on three boats full of Marco's men just now. Two boats turned round and headed for home, but one tried their luck and was dead in a matter of seconds. Now the general and his colonels all think that they will return and it's just a matter of time," I told her.

"Shit!" was all she said, long and slow. "This is really happening, then?"

"Looks like it. So, grab some warm clothes and let's get back down to the den," I instructed.

I grabbed the two blankets from the bed and threw them over my shoulder. Janie, seeing what I did, grabbed two pillows and stuffed them under her arm.

"We need to make a stop in the kitchen for some food and drinks to tide us over on the way," I stated.

"How long are we gonna be down there for?" she asked.

"I don't know. Maybe a couple of days. However long it takes, I suppose."

With our bedsheets, pillows, and bags of clothes, we struggled down the stairs. They were small bags, as neither of us could bring anything from home, and all we had was what we bought in the many service stations on the way or scrounged from the residents there. I had a couple of tee shirts and one other pair of jeans, and Janie had three tee shirts, a cardigan and two pairs of trousers. We didn't stop at the kitchen as we had too much to carry and headed down to the den. We squeezed past Freddy and Thomas, sat at the desk with the monitors, and headed to cell number one.

There was only the pull-down bed. A single bed, but definitely not enough room for two to sleep on. I looked at Janie and she looked disappointedly at me.

"Ok, I'll see what dad can suggest. He knows this place better," I said.

I left her to look at our new home for the next few days and consulted my father.

"Dad, there's only one bunk in there. Do you have another double bunk or something?"

"Oh, shit, yes. Sorry. Um, take the mattress from cell two and throw it on the floor with the one in your cell. I think that's the best we can do, sorry."

"Trust me," said Thomas, "the mattress on the floor is way more comfortable than the bunk, anyway."

I smiled as a thank you to Thomas. I could see that there was no other option at the moment, and I decided to not be any further burden than I already was and grabbed the mattress from cell two and placed it on the floor with the other one in our cell. Janie had already lifted the bunk into its upright position and was out of our way.

"What about the camera?" she asked, pointing at the ceiling.

I could see that there was a wire going into the camera and stood on the stool that was tucked away in the cell's corner. It was a simple click insert, so I pulled at it, and it came away from the device.

And that was that. Everything was quiet from that point. No sightings of anymore intruders or invaders, no meetings in the dining area. Absolutely calm. Things never got completely back to normal in the castle. Everyone remained in a state of readiness, taking turns at their posts and having turns for mealtimes. Two mealtimes a day, in fact, split into two sessions, so everybody could eat a hot meal and man their posts.

Check calls continuously flowed into the control room over the radio, all with no updates. That calm lasted for three days, when all hell broke loose.

Chapter Eleven

We heard two distant yet powerful explosions from inside the castle. Thomas had the fireball visible on the three large screens.

"Sir, that is coming from the East point lighthouse," said Thomas.

The general grabbed the mic from its housing.

"East point; East point, do you copy?" he called.

There was no instant reply. He pressed the button on the mic again.

"Rosemary or Wombat, do you copy?"

The general seemed concerned, as there was no reply.

"Is it possible to get a better angle?" he asked, tapping Thomas on his shoulder.

Freddie raced down the stairs into the control room.

"What's happening?" he asked.

"Freddie, can we get a better angle on the East Point lighthouse areas? You know this system better than me," asked Thomas, as soon as he saw Freddie sit next to him.

As Freddie and Thomas inspected cameras, a voice spoke on the radio.

"East point to control, over."

The general spoke into the mic. "Go ahead East point."

"Yes, control, Rosemary and Wombat are destroyed. I repeat, Rosemary and Wombat are destroyed. Unknown casualties over."

"Received, over and out," the general said, replacing the mic. "Shit! I bet they can see it from Rue point. Why the fuck can't we?" he barked at his two men at the controls.

"Sir, they are higher and have a line of sight," said Thomas.

"We have it Sir, I can confirm we have lost them, Sir," said Freddy.

The screens filled with fire and debris from the Apache sprawled across the grounds of the East lighthouse and the Defiant-class boat leaning into the north sea, held afloat only by its moorings.

"Jesus H Christ. Sound the alarm! We are under attack!" the general shouted.

The sonar alarm rang around the castle, and the warning was echoed across the radios.

"How the hell did they get past the three points?" shouted the general.

"I don't know, sir, unless they came from the Mull of Kintyre straight to the East point. But East point should have seen them, sir," Freddie stated.

"Well, they have certainly levelled the playing field now," stated the general.

A voice came over the radio. "Rue point to control."

"Go ahead Rue point, over," said Freddie into the mic.

"Control, I have four inflatables heading for Doon bay. I repeat four inflatables heading for Doon bay, over."

Freddie looked at the general. "What are your orders, sir?"

The general took the mic from Freddie. "Rue point, this is control. If they are armed, keep us informed of numbers and movement. Over."

"This is Rue point. We counted sixteen men armed with assault rifles and rocket launchers. Mad Joe is preparing to launch eagle one as we speak. Over and out."

I joined them at this point and had to ask, "What is eagle one, Dad?"

He looked at me and smiled. "Eagle one is our silent, back-up air force. Mad Joe puts on a bullet proof suit and mask and flies over the enemy, dropping grenades or balls of Semtex on them from his hand made hang glider. Very silent, but deadly too."

"My God, no wonder you call him Mad Joe," I said.

He laughed. "You'd think that's why we call him Mad Joe, wouldn't you?" Dad said.

"It's not?" I asked.

Freddie turned his head and leaned back in his chair to catch my eye and shook his head with a wry smile.

* * *

Stood on the walkway at the very top of Rue point lighthouse, was sixty-seven years old Mad Joe. Poised in a camouflaged suit and mask, with his hang glider sail catching the wind behind him. With his harness strapped around him and attached to the glider, he held on tight to the control bar

186

with one hand and pulled down his goggles to cover his eyes with the other. He touched the belt full of grenades around his neck as if to double check they were there, and he was ready. Jumping from the walkway, the wind instantly lifted him. The glider dived towards the sea, before lifting higher than the lighthouse towards his prey.

Within minutes, he was over them, circling them like some gigantic bird of prey. He plucked a grenade from his shoulder belt, then a second, and plucked the safety rings from them. Choosing the right moment, he let go of the striker levers and started counting. On three, he clucked like a chicken, and dropped them, then quickly grabbed the control bar and steered away.

The five men and one-woman crew all stared at the noise of the grenades falling at their feet, but before they could react, the explosion blew them to pieces, along with their inflatable.

A second inflatable, shocked by the huge explosion, steered violently away from the blast and pulled to a stop.

"Everybody stop! They must have this area mined," shouted one man in a craft bobbing on the waves. The three remaining inflatables stopped where they were and waited for instructions.

Mad Joe had circled back around and was over them again, unheard. He plucked two more grenades from the belt and pulled the pins. In unison, he released the striker levers and clucked like a chicken. The invaders heard his loud clucking. He dropped the grenades and started away again. Invaders searched the sky, spotting the glider moving away as grenades fell towards them.

"Grenades!" One shouted, and along with his four comrades in arms, leapt from their craft into the sea. Their inflatable blew to pieces in front of them. The two remaining inflatable crew members opened fire at Mad Joe.

As Mad Joe soared away, he could feel some bullets hitting his bullet proof suit. They could not penetrate his suit but hurt like hell. His sail was being peppered by their assault, and he headed towards the castle and hoped he could make it there.

The five men in the water grabbed the nearest inflatable and the two remaining vessels headed towards the beach at Doon bay. With shallow drafts on the inflatables, they easily crossed over the hidden rocks below them. The remnants of their predecessors and the Princess served as a visible warning.

The inflatables buried their noses in the sand. The men from the lead craft climbed out of the boats, stood on the sand, and waited for the others. One man, armed with a bazooka, stepped toward the stairway, carved from solid rock, leading upward. He felt a crunch under his foot and blew himself to pieces all over his friends.

"For fuck's sake! The beach is mined!" shouted one, staying as still as he could in the sand.

Everyone stopped in their tracks. No one moved.

"We can't stay here like sitting ducks, and now they definitely know we are here," shouted another.

"Major, what do we do?" shouted a third.

Major Jerry Francolm looked around at his surroundings. It had been a while since he found himself in this situation. Since his part in operation Red Dawn, (a joint task force with the American 1st Brigade Combat Team, charged with the capture of Saddam Hussein) Major Jerry Francolm had spent his days in the S.A.S. training others to fill his shoes.

"Corporal Lee, can you reach that plank of wood there?" he said, pointing to it at the edge of the rocks.

"I think so sir," He said, throwing his rifle over his shoulder and reaching for it.

"Careful," the major continued. "We can use it to clear a path."

The Corporal grabbed one end of the wet scaffolding plank and dragged it towards him.

"Lift it, man, don't drag it," the major shouted.

"I'm trying. It's fucking heavy, you know," the corporal replied.

With a huge effort, the corporal held the plank aloft in his arms.

"Now just drop it in the direction we need to go and brace yourselves," the major added.

The corporal threw the plank, reaching a distance of approximately three feet. He promptly crouched, positioning his back towards the landing plank. It flopped, almost silently, and slightly buried itself in the sand. There was no explosion.

"Have you done any mine training, corporal?" asked the major.

"No, but I'm a quick study," he replied.

"Ok then, take out your knife, and gently stab into the sand to feel for any signs of metal. If it's clear, move on. If you find one, mark it for everyone behind to see where it is. For fuck's sake, be gentle."

The corporal removed his rifle from his shoulders and passed it to the nearest soldier.

"Hold this for me. I don't want it falling off on one," he said.

He took his knife and crouched down. He gently stabbed the sand, repeatedly, moving forwards slowly into the cleared space. The men behind him stood in his footprints in the sand. After a short time, he reached the end of the plank and stood on it. He turned, smiling.

"All clear major."

It was at that precise moment that a single shot rang out. A sniper somewhere shot the smiling corporal in the head, and he fell lifeless to the sand. All the others crouched, expecting an explosion that didn't happen.

"Sniper!" came a cry from someone.

"Hurry! Walk over him if necessary, reach the plank, find the stairs, and take cover," said the major.

The remaining eleven men scrambled to the steps. The first one to arrive was a scared young lad, barely twenty. He leapt onto the bottom step and his feet immediately slipped off, and he planted his face into a higher step, smashing his teeth. As he slid down the oiled steps on his back, his ass touched the sand, and he, too, exploded into pieces.

The explosion paused the others from forward movement.

"Keep moving, get off the beach," the major shouted.

The last man climbing out of the inflatable was shot in the head by the sniper and then fell into the craft. His bodyweight, falling into the inflatable, unburied the nose of the craft from the sand and it drifted slowly back to sea. The next four sniper shots buried themselves into the two inflatables, with each hole whistling its protest as they deflated.

"Damn it! Has anyone spotted that sniper yet?" yelled the major, crouching on the plank with his men.

"I think he's in the lighthouse, sir. The one we passed coming in," replied the soldier next to him. "That must be at least half a mile away."

The major looked at his watch. "It'll be dark soon. We'll move out under the cover of darkness. Keep alert, men, and keep out of sight of that fucking sniper."

Chapter Twelve

Back in the den, the general was stressing over the lack of air and sea support. Thomas and Freddie scanned as many of the C.C.T.V. cameras as possible, searching for anything out of the ordinary.

"Bird box 3 to control. Come in control." Came a voice over the comms.

The general snatched the mic from its housing.

"Go ahead Bird box 3," he said into it.

"Control, I have troops at my location. Need back-up, over."

"How many are you looking at, Bird box 3?" the general questioned.

"At least seven or eight, over." The voice sounded earnest.

"Received Bird box 3. Help is on its way. Control out."

The general replaced the mic into its housing.

"Freddie, who have we got closest to him?" asked the general.

"We got Marjorie and the knitting club standing by, but they are five minutes out," replied Freddie.

"Shit! This will be over in five minutes. Where's eagle 1?"

"Who knows? He can't reply when he's airborne," Freddie stated.

The general grabbed the mic again.

"Eagle 1, Eagle 1, if you can hear me and are still airborne, can you make your way to Bird box 3's location and give whatever support you can, over?" the general paused as if he was waiting for a reply.

"If there's no reply, he's dead or still up there," Thomas added.

"Send the Knitting club and Bird box 2 to give support," the general commanded.

The knitting club comprised of six ladies past retirement age, three of whom were in wheelchairs. These ladies did not wear uniforms and served as a backup plan. The three ladies in wheelchairs wrapped themselves in hand knitted blankets to keep their legs warm and hide their lethal weapons from eyesight. Each of those wheelchair bound assassins carried a

SA80 assault rifle with an underslung grenade launcher, a favourite of the British army.

Bird box 3 had been in his hide as quiet as possible. The hide, expertly camouflaged amidst the surroundings and dimming light, remained undiscovered by the invaders. Before him, he had counted twelve, and they were all armed to the teeth. It was raining again as the massed invaders began their advance toward the castle.

Brian Johnson, code name Bird box 3, was a veteran and had done three tours with the S.A.S. and was no stranger to facing unfavourable odds. But he also knew that he would lose his element of surprise if he gave away his position now. If he waited, his reinforcements could attack from the front, and he could attack from behind. They would not stand a chance with an attacking force from both sides. But where was his back-up?

He whispered into his radio as to not give his position away.

"Bird box three to control, over."

"Go ahead three." Came the swift reply.

"There are twelve, I repeat, twelve armed invaders moving toward the castle. Where is my back-up?" he asked.

"Back-up is one minute out. Hang in there, three."

"Received," he said, tucking the radio inside his camouflaged jacket pocket.

Suddenly, he could hear a whoosh of wind above him. It was no bird he had ever seen before. It was huge. Then he realized at the same time as the invaders heard it too. Crazy Joe was overhead, tossing grenades like confetti. Three, four, five explosions later, Birdbox three came out of his hide and engaged the remaining invaders from behind. Crazy Joe had taken the full extent of the retaliating fire power; Birdbox 3 had seen his hang glider ditch into the trees, just a couple of meters away. The crash of the glider distracted Birdbox 3 enough to receive a bullet in his arm, forcing him to dive into the hide out of sight.

Twelve invaders had been culled to six. A group of six, including five men and a woman, were determined to eliminate the key witnesses against Marco Dellucci. Their mission to destroy the naval ship and the Apache helicopter had been a great success and had filled them with confidence to complete phase two of their mission; to cross overland and storm the castle with the rest of their army coming in from Doon bay.

Just then, three wheelchairs moved slowly into view. One invader raised his fist and shouted. He was Sergeant Wilson; ex-paratrooper and it was his idea to drop into the shallows from above.

"Cease fire!" He looked at the three old ladies, reminiscent of his grandmother at home. "Get out of there," he shouted to them. But they drew closer still. When they were ten or twelve feet away from him, he addressed them again.

"Ladies, you are going to get hurt if you hang around here. Where did you come from, anyway?"

Six people relaxed, waiting for the wheelchair bound ladies to leave. The shock that appeared on the six faces as the three seated grannies raised their SA80s and took aim at them in unison. Without hesitation, fired upon the six, forcing them to seek cover in trees and over the cliff. The second choice was fatal, as the two invaders who made it perished on the rocks below. After firing the contents of their magazines, the six old ladies withdrew from the scene. The invaders didn't see them go, as they didn't want to raise their heads or offer themselves up for more of a target than they already were. If you asked them, none of the invaders wanted to open fire on old ladies, anyway. Three of them had suffered wounds from the brief encounter with the island's knitting club.

Bird box 3 escaped swiftly from the enemy and reunited with the knitting club. Bird box 2 arrived late for the event.

Wilson waited for a mere five minutes of silence before he found the courage to emerge from his hiding spot behind the ancient oak tree.

"Regroup, with me!" he shouted.

The sole female, Corporal Sally Greenwood, ex-Marine sniper, appeared from the other side of the clearing, helping one of her colleagues to the muster point.

"I saw the Faceman and Bingham forced over the edge," she said. "They weren't as lucky as we are."

She led her injured comrade on the grass and looked at his wound. Wilson saw what she was doing and removed his backpack and dropped it on the floor by her.

"Lucky for us, I have the med-kit. Did you see what happened to Skippy?" Wilson asked.

"He jumped in behind you. Didn't you see him?" she stated.

Wilson smiled. "Honestly, I couldn't escape fast enough when the old ladies raised their SA80s."

"I know what you mean. What a surprise they were," Sally said, joining in with the smiling.

"I thought one of them was my fucking grandmother," said the injured man, regretting the pain his laughter caused him.

Wilson looked for Skippy. "Skippy, where are you?"

A muffled moan came from in front of him. Wilson found him, sat against the blind side of one tree. He suffered a gunshot wound to the leg and to the face. The bullet appeared to break Skippy's jaw and ricochet off the bone, leaving both entry and exit wounds. Wilson helped him hop back to the muster point, where he and Sally patched the injuries of their friends as best as they could.

"Let's wrap it up, sir. Only two of us can still move," Sally said, sealing the man's wound with super glue and her fingers.

"Sounds good to me, but we can't. Our plan is to meet the others from the beach and depart together in their dinghies."

"Let's hope they did better than us, or no one will make it home. Especially, as we haven't even found the target yet," she postulated.

Wilson pushed his jacket sleeve up and looked at his watch.

"it's almost time to check in. Let's see what the major says."

"If he's still alive," Sally added.

Wilson pondered her words. "We'll soon find out."

He removed the radio from his backpack on the floor and keyed the side mic.

"Sun fly, this is Phoenix, Sun fly, this is Phoenix, do you copy?"

There was a brief pause. Wilson was just about to repeat his words when a voice interrupted him.

"Go for Sun fly." Came the voice on the radio.

"Sun fly. I don't think there is going to be a party today. I repeat, no party today. We have eight no shows, two with the wrong shoes, and only two are able to dance. Over."

There was another pause.

"Get to the castle and dig in. Reinforcements are on the way. Over," the major replied. The radio fell silent again.

"Corporal Greenwood, stay with these two. I'll scout the castle and find a good place to dig in."

"Yes, sir," she replied.

Chapter Thirteen

Back in the control room, in our cell, Janie and I huddled together on the makeshift bed, discussing our plans if we escape this situation. Something to pass the time, I guess. Janie wants us to get a place together, anywhere. She doesn't care where. I said I'll ask the general if he would give me a couple of dozen gold bars to buy my castle somewhere.

As new lovers, it was easy to imagine all the things we could do. However, we soon jolted back to reality when a loud bang sounded very close to us. I stood and stepped into the control centre.

"Dad, what's happening? What was that? It sounded very close."

The general was glaring at the monitor screens. "Don't worry son, it was just a basket of boulders falling from the battlements. The rope seemed to snap just as they were trying to place it."

I watched the monitor screens before the need for a drink crossed my mind.

"Is it possible for me to make some coffee?"

The general turned to me and I suddenly realised that this was the general's workplace, and I needed to give him respect in front of his men,

"I mean coffee, Sir," I said, tapping my heels together. But I didn't know why I did.

Upon hearing the heel clunk, Freddy and Thomas glanced at the general, who reciprocated, and all three burst into simultaneous laughter, much to my embarrassment.

"My God Bruce, you are not in the Luftwaffe and I'm not bloody Hitler."

"I know, I'm sorry. Don't ask me why I did that. I was only trying to be respectful toward you in front of your men," I apologised.

"Well, don't. We're all knobs and dickheads here, son," the general added.

"Speak for yourself '*heir General*'," said Freddy in his best German accent.

The general swiftly clipped him around his ear, and all four of us laughed with renewed vigour.

"Thank you for the respect, but you're not force personnel, and I don't expect it from you. No, coffee is off-limits. I'll send one of the boys. You are not sticking your head out in the heat of battle," the general added.

"Thomas?" was all the general said.

Thomas stood at attention. "Coffee for five, coming up, sir."

"You attend to that lovely lady of yours and let us professionals handle the worrying."

I returned to Janie and had time to explain what happened before Thomas arrived with the coffee.

"Sir, the knitting club has returned through the west tunnel with crazy Joe. He looks to be in a bad way, so I sent them all to the infirmary in anticipation of your orders, sir," stated Thomas, placing the tray of coffee and mugs onto the table in front of his empty seat.

"Thank you, Thomas. Take the coffee in to Bruce first," the general ordered.

The general watched Thomas disappear into the passageway leading to the cells. As the general watched Thomas vanish, he heard a voice from behind.

"No one move, or I will shoot you!"

Slowly, the general turned to see whose voice it was. He thought it sounded familiar.

"Major Jerry Francolm. How did you end up on the wrong side?" the general asked.

"General Rankin? You're dead. I went to your funeral," the major said in awe.

"The rumours of my death were greatly exaggerated, major," the general continued.

The major looked puzzled for a moment. A sudden realisation came across his face.

"This changes everything. The safety is now on, and I am holstering my weapon. I whole heartedly surrender. I have no desire to continue against you, sir. Had I known you were our opponent, I would have never signed up for it," the major added, leaning his rifle against the wall, and raising his arms.

"Were you leading the ground assault?" asked the General.

"Yes, I was. We are now down to just a handful because of your force, but reinforcements are coming from Ballycastle. You have about an hour, sir," said the major.

"Put your arms down, major. Freddy, disarm the major," instructed the general.

Freddy stood and ran his hands down the body of the major and removed a phone, a radio, a knife from his thigh scabbard and a revolver from its holster, collecting the rifle as he returned to his seat. He placed everything on his desk. The general picked up the radio.

"Give the retreat command, if you will," instructed the general, passing the radio across to the major.

"Happy to. However, my men here are not the issue, sir. We have to stop the rest from coming across the causeway."

"Well, then do it," the general growled.

"It's not that easy. Dellucci is coming with them. The only thing that will stop him is confirmation that the witnesses are dead," the major instructed.

"Like that's going to happen," replied the general.

Freddy turned to face the general.

"Sir, it could," said Freddy.

"What? I'm not killing my son. Just like before, we'll take them out."

"No, Sir! We fake the death," Freddy said, then turned to the major. "I assume you were going to send a picture as confirmation?"

The major nodded. "Of course. Yes! We just set the scene and make them look dead for the photo. I'll send it to Mr Dellucci, and it should be the end to it," the major re-iterated.

"Should?" the general asked.

"To be honest, Marco Dellucci is a psychopath. Who knows what he will do? But at least he'll have no reason to get his feet wet. I'm sure it will be enough," the major added.

The general paused for thought. "Okay Freddy, you and Thomas make it happen, and fast. See if we can halt the bloodshed."

Freddy and Thomas made their way into the cells. The general took Freddy's seat and faced the major.

"So, what am I going to do with you?" the general stated.

"Well, sir, that is up to you. I will accept my fate. May I provide more helpful advice about your competition?"

"I know who I am up against. I have met men like him all over the world. Continuing this futile attack will lead to the same fate for him as the rest."

"I agree with you. But what happens later on, if Dellucci turns back? When the witnesses are to give evidence in his trial, it will all start again, and then they will not have the benefit of your forces and this castle to protect them," the major instructed.

The general thought long and hard about the major's words. He was right. Of course, he was right. But what other option was there?

"What do you suggest I do, major?"

"When the scene is set, and I have taken and sent the picture to Dellucci, if he continues his attack, then say no more. Do what you do best, sir. But if he turns back, let me redeem myself in your eyes by allowing me to go back to Dellucci and collect my bonus for killing the witnesses, and as God is my witness, I will kill him. I will use the bonus to disappear, and you will never hear my name or see me again," said the major, leaning against the desk.

The general thought about his proposal.

The major added, "Oh, and ensure safe passage for the rest of my men. That goes without saying," added the major.

"Major, we promise not to harm your men, and if they surrender their weapons, we will treat them in our infirmary before they leave my island."

"Thank you, sir. That is kind of you. And my offer?" the major asked.

"Your offer sounds appealing to me, but with one proviso. One of my men, who will bear witness to your actions, will accompany you. If you fail in your mission, my man will have separate orders and there will be consequences. If you achieve our goal, then my man will bring you back here where you may live out your days and replenish the ranks, so to speak, if you should want to," the general instructed.

"You would do that? After all that I have brought to your door. I can see why your men respected you so much, sir. I mean, respect you, now you're not dead after all," said the major.

"You were with me during Red Dawn. I recognise you now that we have talked. Weren't you a sergeant back then?" asked the general.

"Yes, Sir. I'm surprised you remembered. That was a long time ago," said the major.

"I never forget a man that follows me into battle. Besides, that was a good day. Although we were just the scouting party, we located the sneaky bastard for the Americans to claim the credit, as usual."

Thomas passed them and climbed the stairs. The general and the major both watched him ascend. After about three minutes, he descended the stairs with a bag of O-negative from the infirmary.

"You almost ready, Thomas?" the general asked.

"Yes, just got to spread this liberally and we should be good to go," Thomas replied.

"Take his phone with you," the general added.

"Is it alright if I take it and lend a hand? This has to convince, or there'll be no point to it," the major said.

Thomas looked at the major. "Sure. Never done this before," he said.

The major followed Thomas to cell number one, closely followed by the general. Janie and I were led on the floor of the cell on the mattress. Freddy was painting our faces with black paint, making bullet holes in our foreheads. They did not look real enough and looked in desperate need of the blood Thomas was holding.

Thomas passed the blood to Freddy.

"I ain't touching it. Don't know where that came from," Freddy said with disgust.

"I'll do it," said the major and snatched the blood from Thomas. "It's got to be believable."

The major looked around the cell and noticed the tray of coffee. He grabbed one cup.

"Hold this for me," he asked Thomas.

He then squeezed half a cup of blood into the cup.

"You!" the major barked, looking at Freddy. "Mix some of that paint with that blood to make it darker. It needs to be darker."

Thomas passed the cup to Freddy, who squeezed some of the acrylic paint from the tube and into the cup. Freddy looked at the major, who raised his eyebrows to show more was needed. Freddy obliged.

"Hey, do you know how hard it was to come by lamp black?" Thomas argued.

"We'll put some more on the weekly order for you," said the general.

"Weekly. It ain't gonna be weekly anymore, not since the major here destroyed the Apache and Rosemary," disputed Thomas.

"We'll sort it, don't worry," added the general.

"Soldier, Freddy, is that your name?" asked the major of Freddy.

"Yes, it is," he looked at the general. "Are we taking orders from this guy now?" he asked.

"Just do as instructed, Freddy. Their lives depend on it," the general instructed.

"I assume you two are Bruce and Janie, the witnesses?" the major asked.

I gazed up and nodded, unsure how to respond to the man towering above. Wanting to help, after trying to kill me less than an hour ago.

The major crouched down to look at us both at the same time. Janie and I looked back.

"I was instructed to remove your eyes," the major started, sounding sinister.

Janie looked panicked.

"But I'm obviously not doing that now. However, it must appear authentic. So you will both have to close your eyes and keep them closed until we have the photo we need. Blood mixed with acrylic paint will probably sting your eyes. So close them tight until we've finished."

"Dad?" I looked at my father.

"Just do as he says, Bruce. It may save a few lives. Go ahead major," said the general.

The major posed our heads, so that the blood could pool in the right places. He dripped blood from the cup onto the painted holes on our foreheads and pooled it in our eyes, filling our eye sockets, allowing the blood to ooze down our cheeks. He then dipped his fingers into the cup and spattered blood all over us, holding the cup close to our eyes and then spattering outwards to simulate eye removal.

"Thomas, empty the bag where the spillage is hitting the floor. All of it. Equally for both of them," the major instructed.

Thomas followed the instructions and when everyone was satisfied with their artistic talents, the major captured a picture on his phone and sent it to Marco.

"Now we'll wait for the reply," the major said. "Clean them up please, Thomas," he added.

Chapter Fourteen

Marco Dellucci loved his new seventy-five-foot Sunseeker. Normally costing three million pounds, he got this cruiser for the price of four bullets.

The two-man crew managed the Sunseeker alone, so it was unwelcome when thirty armed men suddenly needed transportation to Rathlin Island. The crew had protested that they did not have enough supplies on board for any trip anywhere. Marco's gun across their heads quickly changed their perspective, and they agreed to take him and his men wherever they desired.

While heading to the island, Marco received a picture message on his phone. He studied the message and crafted a reply.

'Do any witnesses remain?'

Marco waited impatiently for a reply, which soon pinged for attention.

'Both witnesses are dead. Mission accomplished.'

A smile appeared on Marco's face. He was in the clear. He would not face a murder trial, but he needed to make sure all loose ends were taken care of.

'Will be there in 1 hr for clean-up.'

He replied to the Major and stuffed the phone back in to his pocket. It pinged again and Marco retrieved it and read the new message.

'No clean-up required. Police expected soon.'

Marco darted his fingers across the screen and sent another message in reply.

'Police will not attend. Expect us in 1 hour with the clean-up team.'

* * *

Back in the control room, the major slammed his phone on the desk.

"The fucker's coming anyway for the clean-up, with a clean-up party," said the major.

"Clean-up party?" asked the general.

"That will be as many men as he feels he needs to remove any trace we were here. Collect the dead and injured. So, anyone who saw us on this island is now a target. Oh, and the police will not be attending. He must have them in his pocket here, too," the major added.

"This guy is as bad as Saddam," the general stated. He paced the floor, trying to decide what to do next.

"What are your orders, sir?" Freddy asked.

I stepped into the control room, wiping blood from my face.

"Yes, what are we going to do now, Dad?" I asked.

The general paced a few seconds more. Freddy, Thomas, the major and I all looked on with anticipation.

"Okay! Freddy, ready the troops. Replenish all stocks and all positions. Thomas sound general alert," the general ordered.

"Yes, sir!" said Freddy and Thomas almost in unison.

The general took the microphone from its housing.

"Colonel Fisher and Colonel Rogers report to control," he demanded, then replaced the mic.

"Major, use your radio to bring your men here for medical attention. Please ensure they are unarmed, or we will shoot them upon entry. Freddy lower the drawbridge and have a security force meet them. Take the injured to the infirmary. Dress their wounds as best we can, then take them all to Bruce's cave."

The general gave his orders, and the room became a hive of activity.

"It's not my cave," I added, putting a bit of levity into the room.

"And what about me, sir?" asked the major.

"Until it's over, you will be confined with your men," said the general. "I will release you after," said the general.

"Sir, I'm sure I would be of better use here," stated the major.

"I don't doubt you. But for now, those are my orders, major," the general stated.

I looked at my father. "So we had all this make-up on for nothing?"

"I'm sorry, son, but it looks like it. I'll need you back in your cell for safety when you are ready, of course," the general said.

"Sir, might I suggest you close the tunnel that I just strolled through as well?" said the major.

"Thank you, major. Freddy, close the east and west tunnels and secure this place for battle stations again, once everyone is in place," instructed the general.

"Yes, Sir," said Freddy.

The two colonels descended the steps to the control room. They stood at the bottom of the stairs and saluted the general, which caught his attention.

"Ah, colonels. I need you two to accompany the major here to help receive his men. Make sure they are unarmed. If you should have any resistance, shoot them. Once they have all seen the doctor, secure them in Bruce's cave, but this time make sure they have blankets, etc. Make them comfortable."

"Yes, sir," they replied and saluted in unison.

The colonels escorted the major up the stairs.

"Freddy, I think we may need some back-up. Who's in charge at Kinnegar Barracks now?" asked the general.

"General Carlisle, Sir."

"Ah, yes. That Scottish twat owes me a favour or two," said the general. "I'll give him a heads up."

Marco tried to insist on beaching the Sunseeker for a swift departure. The crew explained to him that with a draft of almost six feet, he would still have to swim ashore, unless they landed at a pontoon. Marco had never learned how to swim. He had just never gotten around to it. So, beaching it was no longer an option, and they headed for the ferry piers at Church Bay.

Marco had tied the crew together in one cabin to make sure he had an exit strategy, and the Sunseeker would still be there for the return journey back to the Irish mainland.

When they debarked on the island, it was dark and quiet. The locals had retired for the night and McCuaig's bar was the only source of lights, emitting a gentle hum of music and laughter.

"This way, sir," said one of his men, holding an electronic tracker.

Everyone followed the voice in a state of high alert, hiding in the shadows. Empty bottles clanging in the recycling bin startled a few, who swiftly turned, ready to fire. Then, thirty armed men vanished, one by one into the night's shadows, moving east towards the lakes and castle, as if they had never been there. They turned left between a fisherman's cottage and McCuaig's bar and followed the tarmac road.

* * *

At the Castle Retirement Home, everything had been prepared for Marco's arrival. They fortified and manned all positions. All troops received ample ration packs and water, sufficient for a few days if necessary. Everything and everyone were ready for whatever was to happen next.

The islands' C.C.T.V. system spotted Marco and his men, and Freddy and Thomas have been following the invaders since they set foot on dry land.

The general had left nothing to chance and had learned from previous lessons. Bird boxes one, two, and three were fully manned, ready to support the rear in battle.

Chapter Fifteen

Marco and his men had crept silently from the harbour to the brough of the hill, where a white signpost pointed to all the island's tourist destinations. By the side of the signpost rested the Puffin Bus, parked for the night. The bus took the tourists to all three of the lighthouses, and the R.S.P.B. centre at the west point lighthouse.

The third lake they passed, and the smallest of the two owned by the Castle rest home. Their route put them along the tarmac road.

Marco stood looking at the castle for quite a while, trying to see if there was a weakness he could exploit. That was his character, find a weakness in someone and exploit it for his own gain. Bully, blackmail or beat them was his follow-up actions. His actions would be no different in this situation. He had learnt from the best, his father, Marco senior. He was an old school mobster who ruled with an iron fist. If anyone dared to cross him or fail him, it would mean their instant death or a severe beating, depending on the severity of their incompetence. Junior was a lot more feared than his father ever was because he took personal pride in administering the beatings and pulling the trigger himself when eliminating a threat or a witness. No one ever dared to cross him, and he always got his way with things, no matter how stupid they were. The more asinine the order, the more he seemed like a spoilt little brat and thus created hatred and dissention amongst his men, but still too frightened of him to step out of line or do anything about it.

To his men, invading this island, with an unknown number of defenders, with unknown abilities, with just street thugs and paid mercenaries, was as stupid as it goes. Sure, they had eliminated their only attack helicopter and naval patrol vessel, but who owns that sort of machinery? If they could afford that sort of equipment, how well armed were they? And now they have come face to face with a fortified castle. This mission is not going well for them so far. A long-range sniper could have eliminated the two witnesses when the trial goes to court.

The general was not trying to hide the castle. He had all the lights turned on, fully illuminating it against the night sky. The desired effect being that the lights prevented the invaders from using their night vision glasses, but the defenders could. This meant that the first of the invaders to raise a weapon, which was a rocket launcher, was dealt with swiftly, even though they were still a quarter of a mile away. A silent, centre mass round, followed by the snap of the rifle shot, sent the rocketeer head first to the ground.

The rest of the invaders crouched to gain some cover, but a second shot didn't follow. Marco split his troops into two groups. They were to attack the castle from two sides. Each group of men had bright torches that were aimed at the turret walls to good effect, temporarily blinding the castle defenders, giving both teams the chance to approach as far as the moat. It was also easier to avoid the sparse and what seemed like random gunfire. The invaders fired grappling hooks from guns over the turret walls and beyond, then pulled them back until they locked into place.

What the invaders didn't expect was the defenders on top of the walls would quickly tie each of the grappling hooks to boulders. When pulled back, expected to lock into place on the wall, they instead fell and disappeared to the bottom of the moat. Thus making them unretrievable and non-reusable.

Inside the control room, the general was giving orders to suit each new event that occurred.

"Sir, it looks like they are preparing to cross the moat," said Freddy.

"Turn on the motte sprinklers and release the Piranhas," he ordered.

"Yes, sir," said Freddy with a smile on his face.

"Piranhas?" I questioned, just as I stepped into the control room, looking for any information I could gleam.

"It's a fresh water moat so we couldn't use sharks, and our marine biologists haven't fed them for days, just in case," said Thomas.

"Just in case. Oh, that was handy then," I said sarcastically. "And why would you water the lawn at a time like this?"

"I believe the gardening club emptied the sprinkler tanks and filled them with petrol. Just in case," added Freddy, still smiling.

"Yes, and don't forget to remind them they owe me a new lawn when this is all over and done with," barked the general.

I had to shake my head with smiling disbelief and headed back to Janie. It was very boring just sat in the cell, having exhausted most things to talk about. At least with the new pieces of information, there was something else to talk about. I had gotten past the need to point out that killing was not always a good idea and had reached the point where I didn't care less how many invaders got killed, as long as they didn't get to Janie and me. I also knew it was going to be a horrible death being eaten alive by piranhas. That fact still didn't change my mind, but no one was making them attack us.

But I cared about the residents. Some of them had become friends of ours. Those that Janie and I had not had the chance to speak with were still okay in my books because they were risking their lives for us. Often, that is more than most family members would have done. I would have liked to have met the one they called Crazy Joe. He sounded like a right character.

Three of the invaders had swum across the moat and were leaning against the castle walls to avoid being shot at, then down came the rocks and boulders from above, narrowly missing them.

"Okay, Freddy. Light her up," the general commanded.

A single, flaming tennis ball dropped from above and on to the motte grass below, now sodden with petrol. It instantly lit, igniting the three invaders pressed against the walls. They had no choice. As their clothes caught alight, they jumped back into the moat to extinguish the flames, to the waiting mouths of the various sized, hungry piranhas. Their agonising screams rang out for all to hear as the moat turned red in a frenzy of tooth and fin.

"That's it, I've had enough," said the general. "Freddy, put me on speaker."

An electronic beep sounded across the castle, as the general keyed the mic.

"Attention invaders. This attack is futile. Your comrades have already eliminated the witnesses you are here to kill, and your leader, Marco Dellucci, has the evidence to prove it on his phone. If you all disarm yourselves and turn around now, I will not give the orders to attack. So far, we have only defended our positions and yet, your losses have been great. If you leave now, I will free your captured comrades, who can also confirm the witnesses' deaths, and I will guarantee safe passage for all of you back to the mainland. If you persist in this suicide mission, then I will give the order to attack, and with reinforcements arriving soon from Kinnegar Barracks, you will have a very short lifespan." The general paused. "You have five minutes to decide," he added.

Two men immediately rushed to Marco's side. They were Inspector Moffat and Detective Sergeant Wilkinson.

"If they are already dead and you know about it, why the fuck are we even here?" asked the inspector.

"You will do as you are told. I am in charge here and I say we eliminate all witnesses. That includes everyone inside that castle."

"I don't think so. I want nothing more to do with this massacre." He turned and walked away.

"Me neither," said Wilkinson. He threw his gun at the feet of Marco and followed his mentor.

Marco raised his gun and shot Wilkinson in the back of his head, killing him instantly. The inspector turned to the sound of close gunfire and quickly realised what had happened and opened fire on the mob boss. Marco took one in the chest and span to the floor, dropping his gun. The inspector stepped over Marco and kicked his gun away.

"I said no more. This blood bath stops now," pointing his gun at Marco. He made his point clear, and Marco gestured with his hands that it was over.

As his combatant turned and walked away, Marco reached for his gun and struggled to his feet. Standing, he raised the weapon. A single shot rang out from the castle. The bullet exploded the side of his head, and he died instantly. Marco dropped to his knees, and he slumped face down on to the grass.

Several of the invaders gathered together and dropped their weapons in a pile by the side of their fallen leader. A few of them even spat on his dead body. A voice rang out from the castle.

"Please, disarm yourselves and I will send some men amongst you to tend to your wounds. This finishes now. It's over," the general said solemnly.

More and more men gathered together, and the pile of weapons grew. The turrets became full of guards with rifles aimed outwards towards the despondent invaders as the drawbridge lowered.

The prisoners were released from Bruce's cave, and the major took charge of them. The general had his two colonels search and disarm any remaining invaders who thought they might keep their revolvers or their knives. When the situation had neutralised, the general stepped over the drawbridge and stood at the end with his hands on his hips, looking unhappy. He spoke to everyone.

"I will raise a memorial to honour our fallen comrades, on both our sides, and we will always remember their names on the anniversary of this day. We have all, in a way, broken free from Marco and his drug empire's oppression. Now, I know that for every man like Marco that is killed or imprisoned, there will be two more eager to take his place. But for now, there will be peace. What we do from here will be up to each of us individually. But I hope we can all leave, having learnt something from the last few days."

Janie and I stood next to my father. I could not believe what I was looking at. It was like something out of a war movie. Bodies, blood, guns, and I don't even want to know what that is floating in the moat.

But who was that? A familiar face hiding behind some of the surrendering invaders. It took me two seconds to realise why Marco was always so quick to get to us, and he was standing there; Inspector Moffatt. I dropped Janie's hand and crossed the drawbridge. I was so angry nothing was going to stop me. I stood face to face with Moffatt, the reason all this was happening. He could not make eye contact with me.

"Look at me!" I yelled. He did not.

"I said look at me, you bastard!"

I waited until our eyes met before throwing my best punch into his face. He stumbled to the floor. Climbing to his feet, he still said nothing, but wiped away the blood from his nose. I crossed the bridge and took my place between my father and Janie.

From a distance behind everyone, I could see more army personnel gathering with weapons drawn. I nudged my father and pointed to them.

"Ah, late as always," he shouted, "General Carlisle, you out there?"

A few moments later, he appeared from behind his men, and he approached us.

"I didn't believe it until I saw it with me own eyes. General Montgomery Rankin alive and kicking. I was at your funeral, you know."

"Yes, I know. I saw you there. Thank you for the flowers."

"You can bloody well refund me for them. Now you are not dead, that's for sure."

"As tight as ever, I see."

General Carlisle stepped closer and gave my father a big hug. "Come here, man. Bloody good to see you, Monty."

"Thanks, Scotty, but not in front of the men."

A voice called out from amongst the gathered invaders.

"General Rankin?" followed by a few whispers amongst them.

"Still living off your reputation, I see, Monty."

"Jealousy will get you nowhere, Scotty."

The two generals laughed.

"Now, would your men escort these fine gentlemen back to the mainland unharmed, and after, will you join us for a wee dram?" my father asked.

"Why aye, man! Never say no to a wee dram with friends."

"We need to toast to the fallen and plan the memorial," my father said.

"Let us take care of the arrangements, dad. It's the least we can do," I said.

"Okay, son, and thank you."

"No, thank you, Sir." I saluted him and he returned the gesture.

"Is this little Brucie?" said Carlisle.

"Yes, I am."

"My God, you were still on the tit last time I saw you."

"Don't embarrass the lad, Scotty. And please, let's get this mess sorted out first. There will be plenty of time for pleasantries later."

"Aye, Monty. Correct as usual." Carlisle turned to face his men. "Sergeant, get this scum out of here and back to the ferry, on the double."

"Yes, sir," replied the sergeant.

Guards led the invaders away at a jogging pace, and the two generals retreated to the den.

I have never felt so relieved and grateful and proud and a mixture of so many emotions all at the same time. Janie had tears in her eyes, and I guess she was more used to showing her emotions than I was. I kissed her, and we too headed back across the drawbridge and into the keep.

Other books by Steven J Yeo

Keterlyn
Teaching Keterlyn
Queenie Escapes
Queenie in France
Catch 212

www.ingramcontent.com/pod-product-compliance
Lightning Source LLC
Chambersburg PA
CBHW050440200726
48295CB00024B/774